A Nice Day for a Greek Wedding

Debbie Ward

Filotimo

This word only exists in the Greek language and literally means to honour your friend. Filotimo is not taught to greeks, they are born with affection, generosity and hospitality.

Perhaps the world should be more Greek!

When Andrea and Jack decide to hold their wedding at their favourite hotel, on the Greek island of Zakynthos, their best friends, Elaine and Sid, are over the moon. The four friends all look forward to lazy days on the beach, warm, sultry evenings spent drinking exotic cocktails, fabulous food and the company of good friends. What could possibly go wrong?

As family and friends of the bride and groom start arriving at the Ionian Dream Hotel, things start to unravel. With more skeletons being unveiled than at an archaeological dig, will the wedding actually go without a hitch?

Is Veronica exactly who she says he is? Where does Johnson spend his time? What is Lizzie's dark secret? And has anyone actually seen the "willy fish"?

These, and many other questions, will be answered as you join Elaine, Sid and the rest of the wedding party on an unforgettable, and sometimes hilarious, holiday to celebrate Andrea and Jack's special day.

6 Months Previously

Everyone loves a good wedding and no-one more so than Elaine Carter. So when an invitation dropped through the door inviting her and her husband Sid to the wedding of their good friends, Jack and Andrea, she was thrilled. When she saw that the wedding was to be held on their favourite Greek island of Zakynthos, she was absolutely ecstatic. But when she noticed that the big day was happening in only six months' time, her joy turned into sheer panic.

'OMG, Sid' she shrieked, running up the stairs to her husband who was in the bathroom getting ready for work. 'You'll never guess what's just come through the post'

'No idea babe' said Sid as he carried on shaving. 'Gas bill, cheque for ten grand, postcard from the Queen? Go on girl, surprise me'

'He's only gonna make an honest woman of her, ain't he?' gushed Elaine, clutching the white and silver embossed wedding invitation. 'About bleeding time too if you ask me. Trouble is, they've only given us six months' notice and you know what I'm like when there's a wedding. Anyway, I think I'll tell the girls I'll be in this afternoon and spend this morning booking the flights. Then I'll have to e-mail Christos at the hotel. Then there's the dog sitters and…'

'Whoa, slow down Laney' interrupted Sid. 'What the hell are you babbling on about? Who's making an honest woman of who, and what flights need to be booked?'

'Jack, you doughnut' said Elaine, looking at Sid as if it was completely obvious what she was going on about. 'Jack is the one making an honest woman of Andrea! They're getting married at the Ionian Dream in Zante on September 12th, so now do you see how much stuff needs to be done? Oh and I'll need a new outfit for the wedding, well a few actually as we'll be there for a couple of weeks. Can't have Jack's stuck up brother and his wife thinking we're below them.

It makes sense now why they were cagey about booking for this year. I just hope we can get in. Oh no, it's OK, looking at the back on this invite it looks like Andrea's provisionally booked us all in the hotel and we've just got to confirm with Christos and then sort the flights out.

Actually Sid, thinking about it, why don't you tell the lads you'll be in later as well, this is far more important than work'

Sid finished his shave, wiped his face with a towel and contemplated his day, and probably the next six months that were about to be taken over by "the wedding".

Sid and Elaine Carter were typical "salt of the earth" Londoners. They were both born and raised in Bethnal Green in the East End of London where they lived for many years, before moving to Dagenham, on the outskirts of Essex, when they first got married. Sid was a builder by trade and had worked through the ranks, starting out as a labourer, when he first left school, to now owning his own building company. It was only a small outfit, he employed four other people, but they did very well. Elaine was a beautician, who had also worked her way through the ranks, starting as a Saturday girl on reception of the local beauty parlour to now owning her own salon.

When Sid's building firm really started to take off, they moved to a village just outside Chelmsford in Essex, where Sid renovated the house that they now live in. It was quite dilapidated when they first moved in but two years down the line and a lot of hard graft resulted in a beautiful house that they were both extremely proud of. Having bought the place for a song, and even after factoring in what they spent restoring it, they had made a little over half a million profit on it - not that they ever contemplated selling it, as they loved living there.

The house sat on just under two acres of land, boasting four double bedrooms, three bathrooms, a massive kitchen and an entertainment room which Sid had installed with a state of the art home cinema and sound system. Outside was an enormous patio area which housed a Mediterranean style undercover barbecue area, complete with clay oven and bar.

Whilst he was renovating, Sid built a large extension to the side of the house which Elaine set up as a beauty salon. The reputation she had built up over the years resulted in her now being able to rent space to two other beauticians, allowing her to work the hours that suited her.

Neither Elaine nor Sid ever wanted children so they poured all their money and time into the home, entertaining their friends and family and holidays, as well as the upkeep of the menagerie of animals they had, including two German Shepherds, a "bitzer" they rescued from Zante a couple of years ago, and four cats. Sid also had a large pond full of Koi Carp and a couple of aquariums.

Holidays are a regular thing for the pair of them and they have visited most of the Caribbean islands, India, Florida and quite a few Greek islands over the years, several of which they have been to with their friends Andrea and Jack.

Elaine got to know Andrea when she took her dog to be groomed, at the parlour where Andrea worked in Dagenham, which just happened to be down the road to where Elaine worked as a beautician. They hit it off straight away and have been firm friends ever since. Luckily, when Andrea got together with

Jack, he and Sid got on like a house on fire and the four of them regularly go on holiday together and spend time at each other's homes. One of their favourite places to visit is Zante, where they try to go at least once a year, so that is probably why they were all headed off there to celebrate Andrea and Jack's wedding.

Both Andrea and Jack had been married before, in fact this would be Jack's third time. He had two sons from his first marriage to Diane, who upped and left, leaving him to look after his boys when they were only young. He then re-married some years later to Paula who he met on a rare night out with the lads, but she unfortunately died in a tragic car accident not long after their wedding. Jack swore off women for several years until he bumped into Andrea in his local supermarket. Within a few days of meeting, they both knew they had found their sole mates and, after living together for five years they finally decided to tie the knot at their favourite holiday destination. Both his boys idolise Andrea as she is the mother figure they never had.

Andrea had also been married before to an Italian chef called Carlo who she met on a girls' holiday in

Italy. After falling pregnant with her daughter Sophie and being disowned by most of her family, she flew back to Italy and moved in with Carlo and his parents in a small apartment in Naples. The three of them moved back to England when Sophie was five years old. Finding out she couldn't have any more children was a blow to her and it took its toll on their marriage and they eventually split up with Carlo moving back to Italy. Sophie still sees her father regularly, visiting him in Italy whenever she gets the chance. Andrea stayed single until she met Jack, preferring to put all her energies into helping Sophie to follow her dream of being a chef and into her own dog grooming business. Sophie gets on famously with Jack and both of his boys and they have all now made themselves into a tight family unit.

Getting Nearer

Despite panicking that she wouldn't have enough time to get everything ready for the wedding in September, Elaine soon realised that she had plenty of time and, after the initial excitement of the news, her and Sid settled back into their everyday life until nearer the date.

She spent the entire lead up to the holiday buying various outfits, for both her and Sid and, although they now had a different outfit for every day of the two weeks they would be in Zante, she still hadn't found that perfect outfit for the wedding. This actually turned out to be a blessing in disguise when Andrea asked her if she would do her the honour of being one of her attendants, along with her daughter Sophie and sister Mandy. Elaine was over the moon and, a month or so before the wedding, the girls all went for a day's shopping in London to choose their outfits.

Both Andrea and Jack's favourite colour was purple and it was shades of this colour that they had chosen for their wedding theme. Anita, the wedding planner in Zante, had already sent them over a couple of swatches of the fabric she would be using for the drapes on the wedding pergola and the silk flowers she was making so Andrea came armed with those in bid to match the colours for the attendant's dresses.

After days of searching the internet and then hours trawling round the shops, Andrea finally found the perfect place, a small boutique just off Petticoat Lane that was run by two Jewish sisters who had been trading there for fifty years. Everything was handmade and they not only catered for wedding but also proms, balls and cruises. They had a vast selection of outfits in varying shapes, lengths, colours and prices. The dresses that were finally chosen for Elaine, Sophie and Mandy, were in three different shades of the same colour. Sophie had the darkest purple, then Mandy's was a few shades lighter and Elaine's was a very pale mauve. The floor length silk dresses would also be perfect for posh nights out at home so they wouldn't go to waste and the girls were delighted with them.

The dress that Andrea then chose for herself was a simple, silk dress that just skimmed the floor. The dress had a white background, emblazoned with purple and mauve flowers that matched the colours the three attendants would be wearing. It was quite low cut, back and front, and had spaghetti straps on the shoulders. Although the material was quite clingy, this wasn't a problem for Andrea who was a very trim size eight. It was a bit more than she had intended to pay but they all admitted that, paying that bit extra was worth it as the cut and the way it hung made it look expensive and classy and would be perfect for the cruise that her and Jack had set their hearts on.

The shop had one dress in Andrea's size left and luckily it didn't need any alterations as it fitted perfectly. She also managed to get her wedding shoes there and a stunning necklace that Elaine treated her to, as well as a couple of tops and a handbag for her holiday.

"Oh babe, that dress looks amazing" said Elaine as Andrea was giving them a twirl. "You look like a million dollars. Jack won't know what's hit him when you walk down that aisle."

"She's right Mum" agreed Sophie, her eyes welling up. "You look beautiful, I am so proud of you. Elaine's right, there won't be a dry eye in the place when you come out wearing that!'

"Oh stop it you two, you'll have me bawling in a minute and I'll get mascara all over this wonderful dress. Now are you sure you don't think this is a bit expensive, only it's a lot more than I really wanted to pay?"

"No Mum, it's worth every penny. You get what you pay for, isn't that what Jack's always saying? It's your wedding dress, it doesn't matter what it costs. You don't want Edison and Caroline looking at you like the poor relation, do you?"

"Sod them" laughed Andrea. "Bloody snobs, like I care what they think."

"Edison and Caroline, aren't they Jack's snobby Brother and Sister-in-law?" asked Elaine.

"Oh, you haven't met them yet, have you" laughed Sophie. "Talk about up their own arses, and you should see their son, Johnson, what a prat he is."

"No I haven't but I can't wait to meet them, especially after hearing what Andrea and Jack say about them, but I can assure you I won't be putting on any airs and graces with them. You know me girl, what you see is what you get."

"And that's what we love about you Elaine. Now let's get all this stuff paid for and go and have something to eat in that little restaurant around the corner. I used to go in there when I first met Jack and we used to come up London for a show. I don't know about you lot but all this shopping has made me starving."

Once the dresses were all wrapped up and paid for, Andrea treated the four of them to a late lunch in her favourite restaurant and then, after a very enjoyable and productive day, they all left the restaurant and got the train home.

Mandy, who was supposed to take Andrea's outfit home with her so Jack didn't see it, told the others that she would be staying in town for a bit longer as she had seen a couple of bits she wanted to buy but then decided to stop off on-route at the station bar for a couple of glasses of wine to top up the ones she'd had for lunch. After staying in the bar for an hour or so, she finally caught the train home where she promptly fell asleep. After waking up suddenly at her stop and jumping off the train, she left the bags containing both hers and Andrea's dresses on the seat next to where she was sitting. Luckily, one of Andrea's clients was on the train and recognised Mandy as her sister. After trying to shout after her when she jumped off at her stop, she picked up the packages and took them round to Andrea. To say she wasn't pleased with her sister was the understatement of the year.

Andrea really laid into Mandy, who hadn't even realised she had left the bags on the train until Andrea phoned her to tell her. She told her that if she didn't sort out her drinking she wouldn't be welcome at her wedding, hoping that it might scare her into stopping drinking, at least until after they got back and she could perhaps get some professional help if she needed it.

Andrea had always been close to Mandy as she was the only one of her family that had stood by her when she, and her first husband Carlo, moved to Italy with their daughter Sophie. Mandy only lived about an hour away from Andrea so they saw each other pretty regularly but lately, Andrea was starting to get concerned about Mandy's drinking and this latest episode only added to her fears.

Mandy's drink problem started a few years back, after her, then husband, Rick, got a job working away. Rick worked at a local construction firm when they first married but soon after they bought their own house, the firm went bust and he was out of work. With a large mortgage to pay and debts mounting up, he jumped at the chance of a well-paid job that his mate got him. Working as a "roadie" to the stars sounded glamorous but the reality meant that he was away travelling for weeks, sometimes months, at a time. But, the money was fabulous and he could make more in a couple of months than he had previously made in a year.

Mandy had been working full-time in an office – a job she hated, but once the money started rolling in, she left and got herself a little part-time job working in a boutique just a few hours a week. She had hoped to fall pregnant once they could afford to start a family, but it just never happened. Becoming increasingly down and bored with Rick away most of the time, she turned to drink. Before long she spent most of her day in a drunken stupor. At first she managed to hide it from Rick but he soon realised what she had become. Sleeping with strangers for the thrill was the final straw and he divorced her. Losing Rick caused her to spiral completely out of control and a massive binge put her in hospital where she nearly lost her life. Andrea and Carlo took her in, hoping that this was the wake-up call she needed to start cleaning up her life.

Two years after her Divorce, she used her settlement money to buy herself a flat in a different area, just an hour away from Andrea, where no-one really knew her. She went to college and did some flower arranging courses and started earning a decent living making bouquets, corsages and table arrangements for weddings and parties and also selling them at local markets and fayres. For the first time in years, she seemed happy after finding something that she was not only really good at but that she enjoyed doing. After her stint in hospital she didn't touch a drink for quite a long time but recently Andrea has noticed that she is slowly starting to drink again. Although nowhere near as bad as before, Mandy doesn't drink during the day and manages to hold down her job, but she does get completely legless when out with family or friends or on holiday.

Andrea, realising her sister was starting to get out of control again, had become increasingly worried about her, especially with the wedding coming up but she was at a loss about what to do. It was Mandy's drinking and her latest incident with the dresses which was the main topic of conversation when her and Jack popped round Elaine and Sid's for drinks a week before going away.

'So you reckon Mandy's back on the booze then, do you?' asked Sid as he handed out the drinks while waiting for the barbecue to get hot.

'Well, she started drinking again a couple of years after getting out of hospital' said Andrea in-between mouthfuls of crisps. 'But, to be fair, she did have it pretty much under control.'

'Under control!' coughed Jack, as he choked on his beer. 'If you call being under control, just getting out of your nut at parties, weddings, holidays and any other social event, then yes, she had it completely under control. I call it being a total piss head but, what can you do, she is your sister after all.'

'Yeh, I know' sighed Andrea. 'OK, I admit she has got a drink problem but, as Jack said, what can I do. There's only so much advice I can give her before she goes on at me for nagging her. At the end of the day, she's got to want to change. I can't make her. But I was furious with her the other day when she nearly lost my dress. If Sue hadn't been on that train and brought it home for me, I think I would have gone round there and lamped her.'

'At least your dress is safe and sound, so there was no real harm done' said Elaine bringing out a massive platter of meat for Sid to put on the barbecue. 'I can understand how angry it made you though. I would have gone mental if she'd have lost my wedding dress. Right, enough of what might have happened, let's open another bottle and start looking forward to next week.'

'Sounds good to me' agreed Andrea. 'Although if I eat all that food you've just brought out, I'll never fit into my dress anyway. Who are you expecting, an army?'

Jack cracked open another bottle of prosecco for the girls while Sid stoked up the barbecue and they spent the rest of the evening chatting about the impending wedding.

Andrea and Jack left around midnight and Elaine started loading up the dishwasher.

'Oh leave that babe; we can do it in the morning. Let's just have a cuppa and then go up to bed.'

'It's okay, I'd rather do it now; it won't take me a minute. Put the kettle on while I'm doing this and then we can have a sit down for ten minutes.'

'She's a right one that Mandy, isn't she?' said Sid, taking the mugs of tea out to the conservatory, that was lit up like a grotto with twinkly lights strung all over the ceiling. 'Looks like we might have to keep an eye on her antics when we get out to Zante. The last thing Andrea wants is to have to run around after her all holiday.'

'I know' agreed Elaine. 'It is a worry. At least she's on our flight over so that's one less thing for Andrea to worry about. We just need to keep her away from the bar or they'll never let her on the plane.'

'Blimey, good luck with that then.' laughed Sid. 'OK, enough about bloody Mandy, I'm off to bed. We've got a hectic week coming up, and you haven't even started packing yet, which is unusual for you.'

'You're right, it is unusual. I really need to get my arse in gear and get everything done. Oh and Sid, don't forget to turn those flaming fairy lights out or we'll have planes landing in the garden!'

Sid was right; they did have a hectic week. Well, to be fair, it did fall mostly onto Elaine as Sid worked right up until the day before they flew out. After Mandy's incident with the dress, Elaine had been charged with looking after a lot of the wedding paraphernalia, including the cake, present for Jack, Andreas "old, new, borrowed, blue" items, as well as her own dress and accessories. She also had her and Sid's cases to pack, have her beauty treatments and hair done, sort out cover for her clients in the salon and clean the house ready for the dog sitters to come and stay. She also called Mandy and offered to pick her up on the way to the airport, mainly to keep an eye on her drinking so she didn't turn up at the hotel wasted.

Friday 5th September

The day of their flight came round quickly and before they knew it they were driving round to Mandy's house on route to Stansted Airport. Their flight was at seven thirty in the morning and, as they had to be at the airport by half past five, they left home at the ungodly hour of three o'clock in the morning. After picking a bleary eyed Mandy up at around quarter to four, they got to the airport, parked the car and made their way, via the shuttle bus, to check-in with plenty of time to spare. With the amount of luggage that they had between them, checking in was quite nerve racking, but luckily both Elaine and Mandy had pre-booked extra luggage so they were well within their allocated allowances, or so they thought.

Everything went smoothly until Elaine put her cases on to be weighed.

'No, you're joking, I can't be six kilos over. I even bought an extra ten kilos to make sure I had enough.'

'Unfortunately, the scales don't lie Madam' said the condescending woman on the check-in desk. 'You'll have to take your case over to the excess baggage desk, pay for your extra weight, which comes to ninety pounds, and then bring your case back here to be checked in.'

'Can't I just pay you?' asked Elaine, getting her purse out.

'Do you think I would have told you all that if I could take the payment here? Now hurry along, there's a long queue of people waiting to check-in.'

Elaine opened her mouth to say something but Sid grabbed her by the arm and moved her out of the way of the desk.

'Don't even think about arguing with her Laney, you know you can't win and we'll just get taken off the flight. It's not worth it. Anyway, what the bloody hell have you got in there to be worth ninety quid in excess charges, the lead off the roof?'

'No, I know what's made me go over' said Elaine. 'I put a load of stuff in there for the stray dogs. Before we came out, someone had put up some pictures of a new batch of puppies that had been found on the beach. I was so upset that I went out and bought a job lot of toys, treats, worming pills and collars for them. You know what I'm like when I see them pictures, it breaks my heart.'

'Yeh I know babes, but we could have bought a new puppy home for what you've just paid out.'

'Well, I did think..' started Elaine.

'No, don't even think about it. I think we've got more than enough animals to be going on with. Maybe in a couple of years when I've retired we can think about getting another one.'

'Oh okay' said Elaine, looking downcast.

'And don't think you can get round me again like you did last time when we brought Benji home, because you won't. Now let's get this flaming case checked in and get into the departure lounge.'

With the cases safely on their way to the plane, the three of them proceeded through security and into the departure lounge. After plonking Sid down with a coffee and all the hand luggage, Elaine and Mandy made the obligatory trip into the duty free shop to stock up with perfume and make-up. They had no sooner re-joined Sid and got a coffee for themselves than their flight number was showing that their plane was boarding and they made their way to, what seemed the furthest gate in the airport, for departure.

Boarding took place almost as soon as they arrived at their gate and within half an hour they were in the air and bound for Zante. The flight, at just over three hours long, gave the three of them time to catch up a bit on their sleep, although after about an hour of dozing they were all soon wide awake and looking forward to landing and the start of their holiday.

Apart from the odd screaming child, it was quite a stress free flight and, before they knew it the seatbelt signs were on and the plane was banking over Kefalonia, getting ready for the final approach into Zante.

'Ooh look, I can see the island in the distance' said Elaine, getting excited. 'Not long now and we'll be landing.'

'Where is it we're going again?' asked Mandy, doing her seatbelt up and putting some lippy on.

Sid looked at her as if she was mad. 'Are you for real Mandy, it's on your ticket, it was on the board at the airport and the Captain has mentioned it at least five times.'

'Duh, I know we're going to Zante, I just couldn't remember what the resort was called. Unlike you, I haven't been there before'

'It's called Kalamaki, Mandy' said Elaine, getting animated as she started talking about her favourite place, 'and I'll warn you now, it's not the most picturesque of places but there is definitely something about it.'

'Well there must be as you two keep coming back year after year.'

'Yeh, hundred percent. I can't quite but my finger on it but it does pull you back. It's not a massive resort but there's more than enough for us. The beach is lovely, it's sort of rustic and natural but the thing we like about it, is it's so quiet. Because the turtles nest there and it's a protected area, there aren't any bars, loud music or water sports along the beach. If you want all that you can go to the next resort of Laganas.'

'Well I'm not over fussed about that. I'd rather sit round the pool myself. More importantly are there lots of bars in town?'

'Trust you to think of that Mandy' laughed Sid, 'Yes there are quite a few bars and restaurants, especially down the main road. You've got pretty much all you could want really, even Karaoke if that's your thing. There's also more bars and restaurants at the other end of the resort in the old Kalamaki road but these tend to be a bit more traditional and laid back. Again, if you want loud and in your face then go to Laganas'

'Don't forget all the lovely bakeries and gift shops as well' added Elaine, her mouth watering as she thought about the wonderful Greek delicacies she would be sampling over the course of the fortnight, 'I think you'll like it. To be honest, there's not much to dislike. We've tried a lot of the restaurants out but there are still a few that we want to visit. I added you to my Facebook page didn't I Mandy?'

'The one with all the food on it? What is it, Eating out in Zante or something?'

'That's the one. I added you to it so you could see the sort of places that are in the resort.'

'Oh I suppose you'll be taking photos of everyone's dinner now!'

'The people have a right to know what food is out there' laughed Elaine. 'Right, who wants a mint, I don't know about you but my ears are popping like made, we must be almost down'

They finally landed just after twelve thirty local time, to an air temperature of thirty degrees centigrade. The heat hit them as they walked down the steps onto the tarmac and the awaiting busses that would take them to the terminal.

'Blimey, it's a bit hot, isn't it?' said Mandy, fanning herself with her passport. 'I hope we get through here quick, I'm gagging for a drink.'

Elaine looked at Sid, rolling her eyes up to heaven.

'You don't want to be drinking too much in this heat Mandy, it'll dehydrate you. You'd be best waiting until the evening when it's cooler and just drink water during the day, at least until you get used to this heat.'

'Water' exclaimed Mandy, looking horrified. 'I was thinking more of a large vodka and lemonade. I tell you what, I'll put some ice in it and that will be my water intake. Can't say fairer than that! Right can you look out for my case; I just need to pop to the ladies.'

'She's going to be trouble that one' said Sid, after Mandy had headed off to the loo.

'Oh she'll be alright. We just need to keep an eye on her and make sure she doesn't get too legless. To be honest, she's not really our problem but it's not fair on Andrea to have to worry about her just before her wedding. Once the big day is over though, she can get as pissed as she wants. Now, that looks like one of our cases that's just come round, I'd better grab a trolley'

Once all the cases had been safely retrieved off the conveyor belt, they made their way through customs and out of the airport where they grabbed a taxi for the five minute drive to the Ionian Dream, which would be their base for the next fortnight and the venue for Andrea and Jack's wedding.

The Ionian Dream was a smallish, family run hotel with just over sixty rooms, all of which were beautifully furnished in the typical Greek style of blue and white and came with extra touches, such as fresh flowers and bowls of fruit in every room and baskets of toiletries in the bathrooms. Along with the standard twin and double rooms, the hotel also had half a dozen suites with private gardens, and a separate luxury villa with a small private pool. It also boasted a large bar, restaurant and separate breakfast room and snack bar, along with a large pool set within spacious, well-manicured gardens, which included an area exclusively for weddings.

The hotel was owned by Christos and Anna Stephanidis, who looked after the general running of the hotel, including the meeting and greeting of their guests as they arrived. They were also helped by their son Petros and daughter Eleni, along with their respective partners, Anita and Lambros.

Elaine and Sid had been coming out here for several years now and had got to know the family very well. It was also where they first met Andrea and Jack, who had only stayed at the hotel due to a mix up with the travel company one year.

As they pulled up outside the hotel, Elaine could see Jack standing by the top of the steps and started waving at him to get his attention. He and Andrea had flown out the day before so were already at the hotel waiting for them. The rest of the wedding guests would be arriving in dribs and drabs over the next few days.

As soon as he saw her he called over to Andrea and they both came down and helped them with their countless cases and bags.

'Flipping hell Elaine' puffed Jack as he staggered up the steps with two of her cases. 'How long was you thinking of staying here for? I thought Andrea could pack for England, but you two are off the scale!'

'Oh don't talk to me about packing' said Sid, 'you wouldn't believe the amount of stuff she's brought with her. I mean, how many shoes can one woman possibly wear at any given time?'

'I like to have a choice, and anyway you don't understand, there are shoes for walking, shoes for dancing, daytime shoes, evening shoes, going out for the day shoes, sitting down for a long while shoes. It's alright for you, a pair of flip flops for the

35

day and a pair of sandals for the evening and you're done. Tell him Andrea'

'Elaine's right Sid, a girl can never have too many pairs of shoes. You're both fighting a losing battle here so you might as well give up while the going's good. Right, I hope you don't think I'm being rude but I'm just going to pop back to the bar to finish my lunch before it gets cold and I'll see you all back down here later when you've unpacked.'

'No problem babe' said Elaine, giving her friend a hug. 'It won't take me long to unpack all this lot and we'll be down for some lunch ourselves.'

The hotel owners, Christos and Anna, were waiting for them when they got to the reception desk and immediately came round and hugged Elaine and Sid, obviously very happy to see their repeat guests.

Although Christos and Anna were both in their sixties, neither of them looked their age and both of them could keep up with even the youngest members of staff. They were a good looking couple. Christos was tall and well-built, although not fat, with a mass of greying hair and piercing blue eyes that sparkled when he smiled, which was most of the time as he was a very jovial person. Anna was tall like Christos but very willowy and elegant. Always stylishly dressed and with her graceful demeanour and elegant good looks she quite often reminded people of Audrey Hepburn, although after a few drinks she would let her hair down and party with the best of them.

'Kalispera my friends, it's so good to have you back again. Can you believe another year has come around? Where does the time go?'

'Well it doesn't look at thought time has caught up with you Anna' said Sid, kissing the owner's wife on her cheeks. 'I swear you look younger every year we come.'

'Oh get away with you Sid. Stop making an old woman blush. You know it makes Christos jealous when you flirt with me like this'

'Yes Sid, every year you tell my wife she gets more beautiful. How come you never tell me I get more handsome?' Christos laughed and hugged his good friend, after going through the greeting that they have every year.

After exchanging more friendly banter and hugs, Elaine and Sid finally managed to get checked in and Jack helped them carry their cases to their rooms. Elaine and Sid's room was a few doors along from Mandy's, on the top floor. This was the room that they had every year as it afforded them stunning views over farmland to the sea. While Mandy dumped her case in her room and headed straight back down to the bar, Elaine and Sid unpacked the majority of their stuff before changing into some swimwear and going to join the others.

Mandy was already on her second vodka and lemonade by the time they all met up, much to Jack's disapproval.

'Bloody hell Mandy, you've only been here five minutes, they're not going to run out of vodka anytime soon. Why don't you slow down and get something to eat?'

'Oh leave her alone Jack' whispered Andrea. 'If she wants to get drunk and miss coming out with us this evening because she's flaked out in her room, so be it. I'm past trying to tell her what to do. It only goes in one ear and out the other so you may as well save your breath. Now what are you two having?'

'I know what I'm having' said Elaine without even looking at the menu.

'Don't tell me' said Sid, taking the menu off her. 'A Caesar salad with bacon and chicken and a bottle of that lemon lager.'

'How do you know that?'

'Because it's the same thing you have for your first lunch every time we come out here.'

'Yeh I suppose it is a bit predictable' agreed Elaine. 'But they do make the best Caesar salad I've ever tasted. So, what are you having then?'

'I don't know' said Sid perusing the menu. 'I think I might have one of those Gyros and some chips. What about you Mandy?'

'Oh, I don't want anything; I ate on the plane coming over. But I'll have another vodka if anyone's offering?'

'Mandy, you had a small tub of Pringles on the plane, that's hardly going to fill you up. Why don't you have a Greek salad or something if you're not that hungry?'

'Egh! No thanks, I think I'll stick to the vodka if it's all the same to you. Right, no offence but I'm going to sit up the bar and chat to the barman while you and Elaine have your lunch. See you in a little while.'

The others watched her get up and walk over to the bar to order yet another vodka. Jack went to say something but Andrea stopped him mid-flow.

'Don't. I said earlier that I'm past caring what my sister does and I mean it. Let her get on with it. She's not going to stop us enjoying ourselves, now forget about her.'

Jack nodded in agreement and the conversation moved to where they were going to eat that evening. This was before they had even ordered their lunch but was the usual for the four friends whose main topic of conversation, more often than not, evolved around food and restaurants.

Once Elaine and Sid finished their lunch the four of them moved round to the pool and had a couple of hours sunbathing. The pool area at the Ionian Dream was extremely eye catching with a large lagoon style pool taking centre stage and the space around it consisting of both tiled and decked sections. The gardens at the back of the pool area were mainly laid to lawn with palm type trees and stunning bougainvillea dotted around. There were sun loungers and umbrellas set out in both in the gardens and around the pool, with large sofas and tables on the decked areas. The four friends caught up with a bit of sleep before going back to their rooms to get ready for that evening. Elaine and Sid felt much more human after they had showered and changed and, after finishing their unpacking and catching up with Facebook for half an hour on their balconies, they met Andrea and Jack in the bar for the first cocktail of the holiday. As predicted, Mandy was too drunk to go out and spent the evening flaked out in her room. The others decided to eat in the hotel as they all agreed they could do with a fairly early night in readiness for a full day on the beach the next day.

Xanadu, the hotel restaurant, run by the owners' daughter Eleni and her husband Lambros, was chic but still cosy, serving up traditional Greek food with a twist. Eleni, who did most of the cooking and who was trained under one of the best chefs in New York, along with her husband Lambros, a handsome Greek who could charm the birds from the trees, made a formidable team and had put the restaurant on the map as one of the most popular on the island. Its great reputation meant that it was enjoyed, not only by hotel guests, but by locals who travelled miles to use it. It was also one of Elaine and Sid's favourite restaurants on the island so they were more than happy to eat there when Andrea and Jack suggested it.

Lambros was the first to greet them when they walked through the door, kissing the ladies in the way that only the Greeks can do, and shaking the men's hands.

'Hey, my friends, Kalispera, it's good to see you again. Welcome to Xanadu, come and sit down over here, the best table in the house, just for you.'

'Hello Lambros' said Sid, shaking his hand. 'It's good to see you again. How's that gorgeous wife of yours?'

'Ah, you only say that so she will give you extra Moussaka.'

'Absolutely, but don't forget the extra Baklava she plies me with too.'

'Oh my god, I didn't know she did this. Now it gets serious' laughed Lambros. 'So how long are you here for?'

'Two weeks, as always. A fortnight of sun, sea and silliness. But this time, we'll be celebrating this lovely couple getting married'

'Ah, of course' said Lambros. 'Petros and Anita have been going on about it for weeks. I think it will be a good day.'

'Well I hope so' nodded Andrea. 'Everything's organised and in Petros and Anita's capable hands so all we need now is to get all the family here safe and sound and pray that they all get on.'

'Unfortunately, family is something we cannot organise. They will do as they want, as most families do. But I'm sure it will be fine when they get here.'

The looks on Andrea and Jack's faces didn't quite convince him.

After a couple of rather strong cocktails, thoughts of family feuds were long forgotten and the four of them had a very enjoyable evening, with great food and even better company. Once they had worked their way through a selection of dips and pitta to start and then fillet steaks for the boys, seafood risotto for Andrea and lamb chops for Elaine, they enjoyed some fresh filter coffee before saying their goodbyes and making their way upstairs to their beds.

Saturday 6th September

After a wonderful nights' sleep, Elaine and Sid woke up feeling refreshed and ready for the day ahead. They quickly got washed and dressed and went downstairs for breakfast which was served in a large sunny room, that spilled out onto a poolside veranda. The breakfast itself was buffet style and consisted of a selection of fruit, pastries, meats and cheeses as well as a good selection of hot food, including fried and scrambled eggs, bacon and sausages. Pots of piping hot tea and coffee, as well as the obligatory toast machine, completed the set up.

They walked through the breakfast room and found Andrea and Jack sitting at their regular table out on the large veranda, already half way through a full English.

'Blimey, couldn't you two sleep?' said Sid as he plonked himself down at their table while Elaine went and got them a couple of coffees from the buffet that was inside in the breakfast room.

'Yeh, we had a great night's sleep' said Jack in between mouthfuls of egg and bacon, 'but I can't be doing with staying in bed when the weather's this good. I can always have a kip on the beach if I get tired later on.'

'No, I make you right mate, I'll definitely be getting my head down on that beach this afternoon, especially after a couple of beers at with lunch.'

Elaine returned from the breakfast room with two black coffees and a plate full of toast, complete with butter and assorted jams and marmalades.

'You've got her well trained Sid' laughed Jack as he dodged a pat of butter that Elaine lobbed at him.

'Obviously not well enough though as she's forgotten the egg and bacon I asked for.'

'Very funny' said Elaine. 'You can go and get the lunches at the beach for that'

'Actually, it would be nice for you two to wait on us for a change' laughed Andrea, noticing the horrified expressions on Jack and Sid's faces. 'We're on holiday as well you know. You're not the only ones that go to work.'

'You don't call that work do you Andrea?' teased Sid. 'Bathing dogs and brushing their fur for them, not proper work, is it Jack?'

'I'm staying out of this mate and so should you if you value your manhood. She's got a hefty kick for a little'un. Oh God look at the state of that!'

They all turned to where Jack was looking just in time to see Mandy tottering out from the breakfast room, with a black coffee and even blacker sunglasses on.

'Oh ha, ha, very funny' said Mandy, pulling up a chair at the table behind them. 'Sorry I didn't make it last night, I think I might have eaten something dodgy, as I was rough as anything all night'

'Mandy, you didn't eat anything yesterday, apart from a tub of Pringles. You don't think it might have had something to do with the double vodkas you were chucking down your neck as soon as you got here.'

'That's it Andrea, blame the booze. I might have been really ill last night for all you care.'

'Yeh and pigs might fly. I've told you, if you want to drink yourself to death that's up to you but don't lie about it and blame everything and everyone for your inability to say no. Right, we're going back to the room to get our stuff for the beach, I take it you will be staying round the pool today?'

'I thought I might, just in case I feel like I need to go and have a lie down'

'Whatever!' said Andrea, infuriated with her sister's attitude, 'I'll see you later when we get back. If you're still sober that is.'

Andrea and Jack got up and made their way back to their room, closely followed by Elaine and Sid, leaving Mandy sitting round the pool with her coffee.

After applying sun cream, packing beach bags and having last minute ablutions, the four of them met in reception and started walking down to the beach. It was a pleasant ten minute stroll through beautiful countryside to get to the sea. On the way there, they stopped off and bought a couple of brightly coloured air beds for the girls, an extortionately priced English newspaper for Sid and Jack to catch up with the football news and a couple of large bottles of water straight from the freezer.

'You really shouldn't let Mandy get to you like that Andrea' said Jack as they laid their towels out on the sun beds that were only feet from the sea that was gently lapping against the shore.

'I know I shouldn't' said Andrea slipping her beach dress over her head and tying her hair back, 'I know she's my sister and I love her dearly, but the woman infuriates me with her selfishness. It's always about her all the time and I get sick and tired of hearing the same old thing. It's like a stuck record. But hey, ho I'm not going to let her spoil my holiday if it kills me. Or I kill her first.'

'Right you two' said Sid flinging off his t-shirt, 'last one in buys dinner tonight'

All four of them ran into the sea, where they spent the next half an hour or so chilling out in the clear, warm waters of the Mediterranean before spending the rest of the morning either reading, listening to music or sleeping. Before they knew it, their stomachs were rumbling and Sid was nominated to go and get them some lunch from Spiros, the guy

49

who sold sandwiches, burgers and salads from his mobile catering van at the entrance to the beach.

About three quarters of an hour later, Sid returned with a carrier bag full of food and a tray of teas and coffees.

'Bloody hell Sid, where on earth have you been? You've been gone ages' said Elaine, getting up from her sun bed and taking the bag off Sid.

'Oh, you know what Spiros is like' said Sid, putting the umbrella up so they could eat their lunch in the shade. 'He had to update me with all his news since last year and then Ria came down to help him and I had a chat with her and made a fuss of the dogs. But anyway, I'm here now, better late than never. Mine's the bacon baguette Laney, by the way, seeing as I never did get my fry up this morning'

They all tucked into their lunch, sitting under the umbrellas chatting for a while until their food had gone down. Then, after having a swim, they all laid out in the sun to dry and have a snooze.

Although asleep, Sid soon became aware of someone watching him and slowly opened his eyes to find one of the African "lookie lookie" men standing over him with a hand full of brightly coloured braids.

'You want me to braid your hair, Sir?'

Sid looked at him in astonishment.

'Are you having a laugh mate?'

'No Sir, I have very nice braids, very cheap for you today.'

'I'm sure you have mate but have you noticed that I actually haven't got any hair' said Sid running his hand over his close cut shaved, balding head.

'I tell you what though. If you can get even one of your braids into my hair, then I'll eat the rest of them.'

Sid could see the others doubling up with laughter and realised that he had been set up. Even the "lookie lookie" man was now laughing.

'Very good joke Sir.'

'Oh yes very funny. OK which one of you lot put him up to it. I can't help being phallically challenged you know. Now what are you laughing at?'

It took a minute or so for the others to stop laughing long enough to tell Sid what was so hilarious.

'You plonker, it's follically challenged not phallically challenged' said Elaine between laughs. 'You do know the difference between the two of them, don't you?'

'Oh that's it, all take the piss out of me, why don't you. What is it; have a go at Sid day?'

'Actually mate you could be right' said Jack. 'Be like Sid. Get your challenges right. Learn the difference between your hair and your willy!'

'Well, all I can say is I'm glad I've kept you lot all entertained today. I'll be coming round with a hat later.'

'Make sure you remember where to put it, mate' said Jack as the other's started laughing again.

The "lookie lookie" man stood there looking totally bemused and eventually walked off down the beach shaking his head at the crazy English tourists.

They spent the rest of the afternoon in and out of the sea, until about 4.30 when they dried off, got their stuff together and started to make their way back to the hotel, stopping only at Spiro's to leave the airbeds at the back of his van ready for the next time they came down to the beach. Once back at the hotel, they had a quick coffee in the poolside bar before going to their respective rooms to get ready for the evening.

Elaine and Sid were the first down to the bar and Sid ordered a pina colada for Elaine and a pint of Mythos for himself. They sat up at the bar chatting to Christos and Anna's son, Petros and his cousin Alex who helped him run the bar. Petros, who had just turned 40, was blessed with his mother's good looks and his father's personality. He was jovial and entertaining, always chatting and having a laugh with the customers whilst working hard and keeping his eye on the ball. His cousin Alex was an amiable lad who worked during the day as a plumber. He worked in the bar a few nights a week to help out the family and also to supplement his income as he had just got engaged to his childhood sweetheart.

Petros was overjoyed to see Elaine and Sid and was full of questions about what they had been doing since they last met. He was also enthusing about the forthcoming wedding as it was his wife

Anita who was the hotel's wedding planner, with Petros helping out when they were busy.

Petros had been married to Anita for nearly twenty years. They met when Anita, who was originally from Kent, came to Zante on a girls' holiday. They have two sons, both at college in Athens.

Halfway through their conversation, Andrea and Jack came down and joined them, ordering a round of drinks and sitting themselves up at the bar with their friends.

'Has anyone seen Mandy on their travels?' asked Andrea as she sipped her Blue Lagoon. 'Only I rang her room when we got back this afternoon and there was no reply, or from when we knocked on her door as we were coming out. She's either not there or just not answering.'

'Have you tried her mobile?' asked Elaine.

'Yeh, I tried it just now and it went straight to voicemail. I'll give it another go in a little while.'

'Oh you know what Mandy's like, she either had a skin full lunchtime and is sleeping it off or she's in a bar somewhere getting off her head. Either way, you know it's going to involve alcohol.'

'I know Jack, but, you know me, I still worry. But I'm sure she's OK. As you said, she's most probably getting trolleyed somewhere.'

'I'm sorry but I couldn't help overhearing' said Petros, handing them all shots of some weird green concoction, 'but this Mandy you're talking about, is she about this height' as he put his hand up to just past his shoulder, 'very skinny with dark hair and wearing dark glasses, even indoors.'

'That sounds like my sister' laughed Andrea, 'why have you seen her recently?'

'Oh, I didn't know she was your sister, Andrea. Yes, she was in here all afternoon with another couple of women, I think they were all going off to Laganas for the evening. I must admit she did look a bit unsteady. The other two ladies, you may have seen them here they come every year from Scotland, well they looked fine so I think she will be OK with them.'

'I know the two you mean, Maggie and Susan. I've got a feeling they are next door neighbours back in

Scotland. If I remember rightly, they lost their husbands in a tragic car accident on a golfing holiday a couple of years ago and now they come out here together, so she should be fine with them, they seem sensible enough. Right, I'm starving, where are we eating tonight?'

'I don't mind' said Sid, necking the last of his beer. 'What about The Sunset Grill, they do a mean Kleftico and their cocktails are pretty good as well.'

'Sounds like a plan' said Andrea finishing her drink and grabbing her bag, 'See you later Petros, no doubt we'll be back later for a night cap or two.'

The Sunset Grill was about a fifteen minute walk from the hotel, down a side street, nestled amongst some olive trees, making it a very traditional taverna to look at. The food was certainly not for the faint hearted or for vegetarians as it consisted mainly of meat cooked to order on the massive barbecue that graced the front of the taverna, along with some of the more authentic Greek dishes served in the pot, such as moussaka and giovetsi and of course Sid's favourite, lamb kleftico. The two couples had been going to this taverna for several years now and had become quite good friends with the owner George, whom they now saw bounding over to greet them as they were being seated.

'Ah, Kalispera, my dear friends it's great to have you back. How are you all?'

'Poli Kala, esis?' asked Jack, showing off his limited Greek whilst pulling a chair out to let Andrea sit down.

'Good, yes I am very well too my friend. Are you here for two weeks as usual?'

'Yes, we are' said Andrea, taking the menu from him. 'In fact we are over here to get married. It's at the Ionion Dream on Friday. Perhaps you could pop along when you've finished and bring that elusive wife of yours with you.'

'That would be wonderful and I will definitely ask Veronica to come as well as it would be lovely for you to finally meet her. As you know, she rarely comes to the restaurant as she works quite late in her jewellery shop in Zante Town, but I'm sure I can persuade her to come and celebrate the wedding of my two dear friends'.

'It would be nice to meet her at last. We always seem to miss her, the few nights she does come in the restaurant. You say she has a jewellery shop in town; perhaps I could pop in and see her when I go there. Where abouts is it, George?'

'It's just round the corner to the main square, opposite the Alpha Bank. It's called Veronica's and she sells jewellery that she makes herself, as well as other trinkets, bags and that sort of thing. Go in and introduce yourself, I often talk about you so she should know who you are but I will tell her about the wedding tonight when I get home.'

'She's not Greek, your wife is she George?' asked Elaine, 'Didn't you say she was Australian?'

'Yes, she's from Melbourne originally. She came out to Zante to get over the death of her first husband and we met and fell in love and have now been married for over 10 years.'

'Actually we have a couple coming out here for the wedding that live in Melbourne' said Jack. 'They are old friends of Andreas that moved out there years ago. In fact it will be the first time I've even met them. It's only because they're staying in the UK at the moment that they could come over here at all.'

'Oh, that'll be nice' said Andrea 'your wife will have someone to talk to about her home town. Actually it's Raymond's 60th birthday next Wednesday, perhaps we could book a table in here to have his birthday meal.'

'Brilliant idea babe' said Jack. 'Everyone should be out here by then so we can have a pre-wedding meal for Raymond's birthday. So how many of us will there be?'

'Well, there's us four, plus Mandy, if she's around. Then there'll be your brother and Caroline, their son, Johnson, so that's eight. Then there's Sophie, Jamie and Stephen, as well as Lizzie and Raymond, which is thirteen in total.'

'Unlucky for some.' laughed Sid, not knowing how true that would be.

'Right George, book us a table for thirteen, next Wednesday, the 10th I think it is. I'll pop into town and get some balloons and stuff and bring them over to you for the evening, and could you arrange a cake and some bubbly as well. I'll pay for that tonight then it's out of the way.'

'No problem Jack, I'll book that right away and please do not worry about paying me, the cake and bubbly will be on me, I insist. Now, what are you all ordering?'

They all managed to plough their way through the enormous portions of food that were served up, even managing to nibble on some chunks of water melon that were brought up afterwards. After coffees and liqueurs, they said their goodbyes to George and the rest of the staff and made their way back the hotel.

As they passed the side of the hotel, Jack pointed to something he had just noticed on one of the balconies. The others all looked at what he was pointing to.

'Oh, please tell me that's not your room up there. It's lit up like a bloody Christmas tree!'

'Of course it is mate' said Sid proudly. 'You should know me by now, always like to make an effort with the decorations. Actually, it's Elaine that insists we bring enough lights to light up Leicester Square, I just go along with it'

'I think it looks lovely' said Elaine 'It reminds me of home, you know how much I love my fairy lights'.

'Yeh, don't we just' laughed Jack. 'It's the guests next door I feel sorry, it's like something out of National Lampoons Christmas Vacation!'

'You're all just jealous' laughed Elaine 'At least I won't lose my way back to the room! Now who's up for a quick nightcap before bed?'

They all piled back into the hotel bar, which by now had started to empty out and ordered a round of drinks from Petros who informed then that he had seen Mandy return with the two Scottish ladies and that she had a coffee and then gone straight to bed. This put Andrea's mind at rest and allowed her go to bed without worrying about where her sister was.

Sunday 7th September

The next morning promised to be another glorious day and this time Elaine and Sid were the first to get down for breakfast, with Mandy, who looked surprisingly perky considering she had been drinking most of the previous day, joining them soon after.

'Blimey, the wanderer returns' laughed Sid, coming back from the breakfast room with a plate full of food. 'I hear you went off clubbing in Laganas last night with Maggie and Susan. You actually look OK, considering.'

'Believe it or not, we didn't actually have that much to drink when we got there. Maggie's niece is married to a Greek bloke who owns one of the restaurants there. We had a lovely meal and came away before it started to get rowdy, in fact I think we were back here before you lot.'

'Yeh, Petros said that you had gone to bed when we got back. We went down to The Sunset Grill to see

George. We've booked a table there next Wednesday for Andreas' friends', husband's 60th birthday. You know, the one's from Australia.'

'Oh, you mean Lizzie and Raymond. I haven't seen them in years. It'll be nice to catch up with them again. I know Andrea was really close with Lizzie at one time but I don't think she's seen her in ages. Actually, talk of the devil, here comes my sister now.'

'Well, this is something I thought I'd never see, my sister at breakfast before I am' said Andrea, plonking herself down with the others while Jack went inside to get them some coffee.

'I can do it sometimes you know' laughed Mandy. 'Actually, you look rougher than I do this morning. Late night was it?'

'No, believe it or not, it wasn't and I didn't have a lot to drink, although to be fair I wish I had now, it might have knocked me out'

'Blimey, that sounds ominous' said Sid as Jack sat down with their coffees. 'What have you been up to now, keeping your lady wife to be up at all hours?'

'If only' said Jack looking equally as rough as Andrea. 'Our bloody air conditioning unit developed a squeak not long after we got in and, try as we might, we couldn't get to sleep. So we turned it off, then we woke up baking hot so turned it back on again. Then the squeak got louder so we turned it off and opened the window and then the sodding bloke next door, who also had his window open, was snoring so loudly I thought he must have brought a warthog back to his room!. So we are both bloody knackered as we must have only had a couple of hours sleep.'

'I think we might give the beach a miss today if it's all right with the rest of you. The maintenance man is in our room fixing the unit and once he's finished I think me and Jack are going to go back to bed for a couple of hours otherwise we'll be fit for nothing later on.'

'Course it's all right babe' said Sid. 'Don't worry about us; in fact we might as well stay round the pool as well. We can save you a couple of sun beds for later. Actually, didn't you say your brother was coming out today Jack?'

'Oh no' groaned Andrea. 'That's all I need, that lot rocking up when I feel like crap. We'll definitely be going back for a couple of hours sleep'.

'Are they that bad then?' asked Elaine, looking worried.

'Unfortunately they are' admitted Jack. 'I know he's my brother, but him and that stuck up mare he's married to are so far up their own arses it's a wonder they don't lose themselves up there. And that son of theirs, Johnson, well he's in a league of his own. What a prat. Edison has got him out of more scrapes than you care to imagine, he really is a complete waste of space. The trouble is though, Caroline worships the ground he walks on and in her eyes he can do no wrong. To be fair, I only invited them because they're family, I really didn't think that they would actually come. This place is way beneath them. They normally go ski-ing in some place the royals go to or hire a villa in Marbella, so they really will think that they are slumming it.'

'Yeh, and won't they make sure everyone knows it' said Andrea rolling her eyes up to heaven. 'Right, hopefully that air con unit should be fixed now so I'm going back to the room for lie down. You coming Jack?'

'I'm right behind you babe. Just going to grab a couple of pastries for when we wake up. You know I'm always starving after I've had a kip. We'll see you three down here in a couple of hours.'

'OK, see you both later. Have a good sleep.'

While Andrea and Jack went for a lie down, the others finished breakfast and made their way over to three sun beds right by the pool. There were quite a few spare beds around the pool that morning so there was no need to save any for Andrea and Jack, as they would be able to grab a couple when they got up. Elaine and Sid had already applied their sun tan lotion in the room before coming down for breakfast so, while Mandy slapped on the factor twenty five, they both jumped in the pool and did a couple of lengths before getting out and drying off. Within ten minutes, the three of them were laid out in the sun sleeping or listening to music on their iPods.

It must have been around 11.30 that Sid woke up to a commotion going on at reception. He sat up and looked over to see an overdressed, middle aged couple and a big lump of a lad in his twenty's causing a bit of a scene. Grabbing his sunglasses and a t-shirt, he sauntered over to the bar to get some drinks and listen to what was going on. When he got to the bar, he could hear the older guy complaining to Christos that the room they had wasn't big enough and that the décor wasn't up to their usual standards as they were used to staying in five star establishments. Christos informed him that, although he was very proud of his hotel, The Ionian Dream was only a three star and he would not get the same comforts as a five star hotel would have.

The younger guy, who was sweating profusely, started to have a go, saying that where they normally go, the staff would come out to greet them with scented towels and glasses of champagne. Christos just looked at him totally bemused. It then hit Sid, who these people were and he went over to them.

'Excuse me mate, I hope you don't mind me butting in but are you Edison Blair?'

The older man stopped moaning and looked at Sid as if he had just stepped out of the gutter.

'What if I am? What on earth has it got to do with you?'

'No offence mate' said Sid, his back going up at the man's rudeness. 'Only asking a question, no need to be rude is there. I was just going to introduce myself. I'm Sid, your brother, Jack's best mate. Jack said you were arriving today so I thought I'd come and say hello'.

'Oh, I do apologise, I didn't realise. Yes, I am Edison Blair and this is my wife, Caroline and son, Johnson, pleased to meet you. Is Jackson not around?'

'No, but they should be down any time now actually.'

'Surely they're not still in bed at this time in the morning?' piped up Caroline. 'I made sure I let Andrea know exactly what time we were arriving here today. They could have at least had the curtesy to come and meet us.'

'Oh I'm sure they would have done' said Sid, 'only they had a bit of trouble with a faulty air conditioning unit last night and didn't get any sleep so they popped back to the room after breakfast to grab a couple of hours shut eye. Why don't you check in and go and unpack and then you can meet us all round the pool in a little while.'

'Wonderful, don't tell me I've got to unpack my own cases now as well?' said Caroline to Edison, looking like she had a bad smell under her nose. 'I really don't see why they couldn't have picked a better hotel than this to get married in. If it was money that was the problem, I'm sure you could have lent them some.'

'They chose this hotel, love' interrupted Sid, who was now getting quite annoyed with their attitude, 'because it is run by our very good friends and because it is a lovely friendly hotel with lots of charm and personality. We have all been coming here for years and there really was never any question of going anywhere else.'

'I'm sure we'll have a wonderful time darling' said Edison to his wife who looked a lot less convinced of this and was obviously far from happy about being called "love". 'Now let's just get our keys and find someone to bring our bags to the rooms.'

Sid decided to go back to his sun bed at this point before he got roped into porter duties, by Jack's overbearing and snobbish family.

Edison Blair was brought up in Dagenham with his younger brother Jackson and their sister Evelyn, who moved to New Zealand some years ago. He was always the more intelligent of the three and as such their parents had high hopes for him. Edison loathed Jack's East End mates and his "common" ways – himself preferring to mix with the wealthier boys from his Grammar school out of the area.

After getting a Masters at University, he worked his way up through the ranks at different investment houses, finally opening his own firm of IFAs in the city. He met Caroline at a financial awards do, where she was accompanying her father who was a very influential banker. They married when Edison was in his early thirty's and had Johnson soon after.

Before she met Edison, Caroline had a string of jobs, mainly on the reception desks of large corporate banks, where her father had pulled strings to get her in. Once she got married and had Johnson, she stayed at home and looked after her son – something she's been doing for the last twenty eight years. She counts designer shopping as her main hobby – spending more money each month on designer clothes than a small country would need to survive. She has a few like-minded friends, who like her, spend their days shopping, being pampered and doing lunch.

Both Edison and Caroline have always been embarrassed by his working class upbringing and have told their friends that he was born on the Essex borders. They are also embarrassed by Jack, or Jackson as they both insist on calling him, as he is typical East End and proud of it. The only reason they even came out for the wedding is because they were frightened of missing something and quite liked the idea of lording it up over Jack and his friends.

'Jack's brother and his wife and son have just turned up' announced Sid as he sat on the end of Elaine's sun bed.

'Oh, lovely, what are they like?'

'Pretty much what Jack said they were like, right bloody snobs. Should have heard them creating at reception because the room wasn't up to scratch and they hadn't been greeted with hot towels and champagne. Honestly, people like that get right up my nose, who the hell do they think they are? He was brought up in the East End just like Jack, or Jackson as he insists of calling him, but you'd think he was royalty the way he was going on. I can't see us getting on with them at all.'

' Andrea always says they're a bunch of knob heads,' said Mandy putting her book down and tying a sarong round her, 'but at the end of the day, it's Jack's family and she puts up with them for his sake. Although to be fair, I don't actually think there's much love lost between Jack and Eddie anyway.'

'I bet you don't call him Eddie to his face' laughed Sid.

'No, even Jack wouldn't dare do that. I remember Andrea saying that he called Johnson, Johnny boy once; you'd have thought he'd committed murder the way they went on about it. Right all this talk of families has made me thirsty, anyone fancy a drink?'

Soon after Mandy returned from the bar with some much needed refreshments, Andrea and Jack came down, looking and feeling a lot better after having a couple of hours of sleep.

'I take it you've met my brother and his family then Sid' said Jack grinning, as him and Andrea set their towels down on the sun beds.

'Yeh, how did you know?'

'Christos told me as we came through reception. He said they'd been whinging about the size of the room and about not being greeted with champagne and hot towels. I told him he was bloody lucky they didn't ask for a herd of unicorns and a flying carpet as well!'

'I can believe that' laughed Sid. 'I got it in the ear for you not being there when they arrived. I said that you'd both be round the pool later and they could join us but they seemed to be more interested in finding some mug to cart their cases to their rooms. That's when I sloped off before they roped me into carrying them.'

'Oh well, at least they got here okay and we have only got to put up with them for a few days, so hopefully they won't be too much of a problem' said Andrea, trying to convince herself, without much luck.

Luckily the rest of the day went without incident and they didn't actually get to see Edison and his family until that evening when they all met in the bar for drinks before going out to eat.

Jack was just getting a round in when Edison and Caroline walked into the bar looking like they were about to have dinner with the Captain on the QE2.

'Bloody hell, they do know it's only a three star hotel in Greece don't they?' said Sid as everyone turned to look at Caroline, who was decked out in a black and silver cocktail dress complete with diamanté accessories and Edison who had on a suit and tie.

'They do look a bit out of place' agreed Jack 'but that's my brother to a tee, always one to make an entrance.'

'Well they're not coming out to dinner with us dressed like that' said Andrea, 'they look like a right couple of prats. Oh no, they've seen us and they're coming over.'

'Jackson, how are you old chap? We finally caught up with you. Your friend Sidney said you had gone back to bed this morning. Bit too much of the old Ouzo the night before was it?'

'No such luck, it was lack of sleep due to a faulty air conditioning unit actually, but anyway it's good to see you both. Sid said you were coming out to the pool after you unpacked so we waited down there for you.'

'Yes, we were going to have an hour poolside but Caroline had one of her heads. She always gets one when we travel so we just lay on the bed with the blinds drawn listening to some soothing classical music.'

'Blimey, I bet that was riveting' whispered Elaine to Andrea, who was trying not to laugh. 'I wonder how many heads she's actually got?'

'So where's Johnson then? Not coming down or has he gone out on his own?'

'Oh he's gone off for a walk' said Caroline 'He said he wanted to take in the local sights and get a feel for the place. He'll most probably join us later for drinks.'

'So that means he's probably gone off looking for strip joint or someone mug enough to give him a quickie' whispered Andrea to Elaine again.

'No way. Is he really like that?'

'Oh yes, he's really sleazy. Caroline thinks the sun shines out of his backside but Edison's always getting him out of trouble. I can't stand him personally, there's just something about him that gives me the creeps.'

'Can't wait to meet him' laughed Elaine.

'So where are we all eating tonight?' asked Sid

'Well, as we didn't see you to ask, we have booked a table here at the hotel restaurant. You're more than welcome to join us but I assume you will be going up to change first, won't you?'

'Cheeky git' laughed Jack. 'We are changed; this is what we wear to go out. This is only a three star hotel Ed. No-one dresses up here; most blokes go out like us, in shorts. You are a little bit over dressed mate.'

'Yes, I admit looking around we are the only ones dressed for dinner. But we do feel more comfortable dressing like this and I really couldn't imagine wearing shorts to go into a restaurant, so each to their own.'

'Absolutely' agreed Jack. 'If you're happy then that's all that matters, and thanks for the invite but we're off up the town to eat but we can catch up later in the bar for a nightcap. Oh here comes Mandy. Did she say she was coming out with us tonight or not?'

'No, I'm sure she said that she was going out with some friends' said Elaine, waving at Mandy to come over, 'although where she's suddenly got these friends from, God only knows.'

'Hiya, I'm Andrea's sister Mandy, pleased to meet you' said Mandy introducing herself to Edison and Caroline. 'Sorry I can't stop but I've got a taxi booked to go to town to meet some friends. Perhaps we can catch up round the pool tomorrow.'

'My word, she's a whirlwind isn't she' said Caroline as Mandy breezed through reception and out to her waiting taxi.

'To be fair, it's amazing actually that she's still walking in a straight line at this time of day' muttered Andrea under her breath.

'Right, I think our table may be ready, so we'll see you lovely people later on maybe' said Edison taking Caroline's arm to start walking over to the restaurant.

'Blimey, I actually feel underdressed now' said Elaine, looking down at her white capri pants and long floaty top.

'I can assure you my darling that you look a million dollars' said Sid, 'and you Andrea. You both always look immaculate when you go out.'

'Well they take long enough to get ready' laughed Jack.

'As I'm always telling you Jack, getting to look this good takes time and effort.'

'And I wouldn't have you any other way. Right have you two finished those cocktails because I'm starving?'

The girls finished their drinks, touched up their lippy and got their bags. They hadn't decided on anywhere specific to eat so just walked until somewhere took their fancy which, on that particularly evening, happened to be the Aphrodite Taverna located at the top end of the main road.

None of them had eaten here before but had heard good reviews from some of the guests as well as seeing it on Trip Adviser. Elaine was eager to take some photos to upload onto her food site and luckily the restaurant didn't disappoint and they were all really happy with the food that was brought up. Both the boys had Greek plates, which were an assortment of different Greek specialities, rather like a meze, that were so big neither of them could quite finish it. Andrea had grilled sea bream, which was filleted at the table for her by the very attentive waiter and Elaine had a massive pot of moussaka and a side of chips and salad. None of them had any room for dessert and just finished the meal off with coffees.

Rather than go going back to the hotel bar and risking bumping into Edison and Caroline, they decided instead to go to one of the local bars, Above and Beyond, which was situated above one of the many tourist shops that sold trips around the island. It was a very chilled out bar, with background music that didn't intrude into conversations and an excellent cocktail list. It also had fabulous views all along the main strip so was a great place to relax and people watch. Jack and Sid both had a beer whilst the girls tried the cocktail of the day which was a frozen peach daiquiri. They sat for an hour or so, chatting amiably about the day and trying out another couple of the recommended cocktails, before making their way back to the hotel. Luckily by the time they got to the bar, it was almost empty, with most of the guests, including Edison and Caroline, having either gone out for the evening or gone to bed. They decided against another drink and went back to their respective rooms for a relatively early night.

Monday 8th September

The next morning started off a little bit overcast so, after a light breakfast of some yoghurt and fresh figs, drizzled with honey, Andrea and Jack decided to pop into Zante Town to choose their photo album and pick up a couple of last minute bits. They left Elaine and Sid round the pool with Mandy, and Edison and Caroline going for a walk along the beach.

They walked up to the main road and hailed a taxi, asking the driver to drop them by the harbour. The ride into Zante Town only took around ten minutes although it seemed a lot longer as the driver seemed to think he was in the Grand Prix and Andrea and Jack sat pinned in the back watching their life flash before them and wishing desperately that they had got the bus. The photo shop wasn't far from where they were dropped off and they took a slow walk along the harbour getting their heart rates back down after the white knuckle taxi ride they had just endured. Once they got to the shop, they spent a good hour choosing an album and having a chat with the photographer about the sort of pictures they would like at the wedding.

After leaving the photographers, Jack suggested they stop and have a coffee and a piece of cake in their favourite café in the main square.

'Right, I need to go and have a look in that jewellery shop that George's wife owns, Veronica's isn't it?' asked Andrea as her and Jack finished off their baklava.

'OK, do you want me to come with you babe?'

'No, you're alright; I know you can't stand walking round these sort of shops. I only want to get a couple of little presents for Sophie, Elaine and Mandy so why don't you just order a beer or something and stay here? It's only round the corner and I won't be long. Just wait here until I get back. I've got my phone if you desperately need anything.'

'OK, sweetheart. Take as long as you want. Actually let's get this bill paid and I'll wait for you in that bar opposite.'

'Is that the bar that's showing the footie? I wondered why you wanted me to take my time' laughed Andrea, calling the waiter over. 'Normally you'd be moaning if I spent more than five minutes in a shop.'

They paid the bill for the coffee and cake and then Jack moved over to the bar opposite to watch some Spanish team, while Andrea walked round the corner to the little jewellery shop owned by Veronica Liasades.

Veronicas was a very quaint, typically Greek shop decorated in the shades of blue and white that are seen all over the Greek Islands. Andrea noticed some lovely pieces in the window and went inside to get a proper look. It was a very tanned woman behind the counter who looked to be in her mid-fifty's that greeted her. She was quite buxom, with long brown hair that was streaked by the sun but what Andrea noticed most about her was her height. At only 5ft 4ins, Andrea felt dwarfed by this Amazonian woman who must have hit 6ft in her heels.

'Hi there, how can I help you?' asked the woman in a strong Australian accent.

'You must be Veronica Liasades' asked Andrea, 'I'm not sure if your husband has mentioned us, but we go to your restaurant every year we come over. This year we're getting married and we invited George and yourself to the evening reception at the Ionian Dream.'

'Ah, you must be Andrea. Yes George said that you were getting married over here. He actually talks about you quite a lot. You come out with another couple don't you? Congratulations by the way. Yes, we'd love to stop by. Thank you so much for asking. '

'It's our pleasure and yes we come out with our friends Elaine and Sid every year. We're actually having a bit of a do on Wednesday at the Sunset Grill as it's another of my friends, husbands 60th. I know George said you rarely go to the restaurant at night because of working here but I'm sure we'll be there quite late so it would be great so see you for a drink or two then and you can meet the rest of the family.'

'That would be brilliant Andrea. I normally close here around 10 o'clock so I can be at the restaurant around 10.30 ish, which will give you guys time to eat your dinner.'

'Great, I'll let the others know, they'll be really pleased. Now the reason I came in here, apart from to introduce myself to you, was to buy a little keepsake for each of my attendants and I think I've seen just the thing in the window.'

Andrea spent around half an hour with Veronica choosing some Greek style necklaces that she had handmade herself, as gifts to give to Sophie, Elaine and Mandy on the day of the wedding.

She got back to the bar just as Jack was finishing off his beer and, as the sun had now made an appearance, they grabbed a taxi, happily not the one that brought them into town, and made their way back, a little bit slower this time, to the hotel and their waiting sun bed.

'Blimey, you timed that well' said Sid as he pulled himself out of the pool. 'I was just going to get a round in. Did you get everything you wanted?'

'Oh don't ask me, I just sat in a bar watching the footy while Andrea went off round the shops. We did choose our photo album though. The photos will be ready for us to collect a couple of days after the wedding which is quick. I remember years ago you had to wait weeks for your photos.'

'What's that, back in the good ole days?' laughed Mandy. 'Don't just stand there rabbiting like a couple of old women, go and get the beers in, I'm spitting feathers here.'

Sid and Jack went over to get some drinks while the girls all took a dip in the pool to cool off from the now searing sunshine.

'Isn't your friend and her husband flying in today?' asked Elaine.

'Lizzie and Raymond? Yeh, they should be here just after lunch. It'll be weird meeting up with them again after all this time. It's got to have been over twenty five years since I last saw them. We keep in touch with e-mail and the like but it's not like seeing someone face to face. The last time I saw Lizzie, she was a blonde bombshell, all boobs and bum. In fact people used to call her Babs, after Barbara

Windsor. If her picture on Facebook is anything to go by, she certainly doesn't look like that now. Still I suppose we're all looking a lot older than we used to.'

'Well you certainly don't' said Elaine, getting out of the pool as she saw the boys coming back armed with a tray of drinks and some bags of crisps. 'You seem to look younger every year. In fact you could mistake you and Sophie for sisters sometimes.'

'Get out of it' laughed Andrea, playfully splashing her friend but feeling chuffed that she could think that. 'Right, I'm getting out and getting some sun. Don't forget to put some lotion on Jack; you know you'll burn if you don't.'

'I'm fine babe, I put some on earlier'

'OK, well it's on the top of my bag if you need some more, just don't start moaning when you're red raw.'

Jack tutted and turned to Sid.

'Does Elaine keep on at you like this?'

'Yep, and it normally goes in one ear and out the other.'

'I heard that' laughed Elaine, 'now shut up the pair of you, I'm trying to read and all I can hear is you two.'

The five of them spent the rest of the morning lazing around the pool, swimming, reading and chatting about the holiday. After a leisurely lunch in the poolside snack bar, they all retired back to their sun beds and slept for an hour or so, only waking when Andrea's mobile alerted her to a text by playing a very loud version of Smoke on the Water.

'Whoa, what's happening?' yelled Sid as he leapt up from his sun bed.

'It's okay Sid, it's only my phone. It's a text from Lizzie saying they've checked in and are unpacking. I've told her we're round the pool and to come down when they're ready. Have you been sodding about with my phone Jack, only I could have sworn my text alert was Abba and not Deep Purple?'

'Guilty as charged babe. I got totally fed up with hearing flaming Dancing Queen every five minutes so I thought I'd put a bit of rock music on there. Sorry!'

'No, you're alright, I've heard worse. Right I'd better get some coffees to wake us all up before Lizzie and Raymond come down.'

As if on cue, Andreas friend Lizzie and her husband came down to meet them just as they had finished their coffees. After all the introductions were made, the girls sat down on the sun beds to catch up while the lads chatted in the pool.

Lizzie and Andrea had known each other since they started school and were inseparable as children and teenagers, living just down the road from each other. Lizzie was with Andrea when she met her first husband, Carlo in Italy and completely disapproved of their relationship. When Andrea fell pregnant with Sophie, Lizzie suggested that she get an abortion as she felt she was wrecking her life. They had a massive row and, after finding out that her family were as good as disowning her, Andrea packed her bags and went back out to Italy to be with Carlo.

While Andrea was in Italy, Lizzie met and married Raymond, a local lad who had just bought a factory selling electrical components from his former boss who had retired, building it up into the successful business it is now. She made amends with Andrea when she came back from Italy and started seeing them all again on a regular basis.

Not long after re-kindling their friendship, Lizzie announced she was pregnant, and that her and Raymond had decided to move to Australia. It was there that they stayed, building a very successful life together with their son Adam, until a few months ago when they returned to the UK to look after Lizzie's ailing parents.

'I can't believe how amazing you look Andrea. I swear you look no older than when I first went to Australia.'

Unfortunately, Andrea couldn't return her friends compliment as Lizzie had aged considerably since she last saw her. Gone was the bubbly, busty blonde that Andrea knew from years ago and in her place was a dumpy, dowdy woman who looked twenty years older than Andrea. The years had certainly not been kind to her friend. Luckily Elaine jumped in to save her from having to make an insincere compliment.

'That's what I keep telling her' said Elaine 'only she doesn't believe me. You should see her next to Sophie, they honestly look like sisters.'

'How is little Sophie? Actually I suppose she's not so little now is she. What is she now, late twenties? No, what am I talking about, she can't be, she's older than Adam. Oh God, this is making me feel old.'

'Tell me about it, Sophie's actually thirty four, believe it or not' said Andrea, her eyes sparkling as she spoke about her beloved daughter, 'and the proud owner of her own Italian restaurant. She really has done well for herself but it hasn't changed her at all, she's still so down to earth and easy going. You'll see for yourself soon, she'll be out here tomorrow. She's coming out with Jack's youngest son Jamie and his partner Stephen. Unfortunately his eldest son, Luke couldn't make it as his wife's not well. How's your Adam? He must be nearing thirty now. Is he still obsessed with surfing or has Raymond persuaded him to join the family business?'

'No, he was never going to get anywhere with that unfortunately, but he's doing really well too. He's got his own surf shop now that sells everything to do with surfing as well as giving lessons, which is his absolute passion. He loves it and Raymond has finally come to terms with the fact that this is what he wants to do and is behind hipness hundred percent.

Talking about Adam, I do need to have a word with you as he's coming out tomorrow. Raymond doesn't know, so keep it under your hat. He thinks he's still in Australia, but he wanted to surprise him for his sixtieth birthday on Wednesday. I'd have let you know before but he only confirmed that he was definitely coming yesterday as he had to get someone to look after the shop. If it's too late for the wedding don't worry, he can always get something to eat out and meet up with us later'

'No, honestly Lizzie it's fine, I'll have a word with Anita, our wedding planner. It really won't be a problem. It's actually really great that I'll finally be able to meet him and I'm sure Raymond will be over the moon with Adam surprising him. So don't worry about it, your secret is safe with me and, to be fair,

I've only got to keep it for another day, haven't I? In fact, I'll let you into a little secret of my own. We've booked a table for everyone at our favourite restaurant for Raymond's birthday and ordered a cake, bubbly, balloons, etc. We thought it would be a lovely surprise for Raymond plus a way of everyone getting to know each other.'

'Oh, that is really sweet; you didn't have to do that. He'll be over the moon.'

'I hope so, anyway, what have you both been up to? You seriously need to fill me in on what's been happening in Oz.'

'Well nothing too exciting, I can assure you. I tell you what, let's go over to the bar and get some drinks and we can carry on reminiscing.'

The girls asked what everyone was having and went over to the bar to try and catch up on several years of news. When they got back everyone was in the pool so they left the drinks by the beds and jumped in themselves. Within half an hour, everyone was getting on like a house on fire and Andrea felt like she had never lost touch with her old friend. They spent the rest of the afternoon in and out of the pool and finally went back to their rooms to get ready, around five o'clock, arranging to meet in the bar before going out to dinner.

Before jumping in the shower, Andrea phoned down to Anita to let her know that there would be one extra at the wedding in the form of Adam. After chatting some more about wedding arrangements, Andrea finished her call and started to get ready. As Jack had just got in the shower, Andrea started going through her clothes to find something to wear, when she heard a scream coming from the shower. She dropped her dress and ran into bathroom to see what had happened.

'Oh my God, look at me' cried Jack, turning the water off. 'Why didn't you make me put some more cream on?'

Jack was standing in the shower cubicle, butt naked and doing a great impersonation of a lobster. The only white areas were where his shorts and his sunglasses had been.

Andrea took one look at him and burst out laughing.

'Oh, brilliant. I'm burnt to a crisp and all my darling wife to be can do is fall about laughing. Look at me, I'm glowing.'

'Well I did tell you to put on some sun cream but, as usual, you know best. You'd better put some after sun on and hope it goes down before Friday. I don't want you in the wedding photos looking like a beetroot.'

Jack finished his shower and slathered on some after sun that Andrea had kept in the fridge. He was still moaning about how uncomfortable he was when they met the others in the bar.

'Bloody hell Jack, that looks painful' laughed Sid. 'She did tell you to put the sun cream on earlier mate. You really should have listened.'

'Yes, I know. There's no need for you to keep telling me as well and yes it is bloody painful so get me a large Vodka to numb the pain!'

After having a couple of drinks, Jack started to forget about his sun burn and they all decided to eat in the hotel restaurant that evening as Lizzie and Raymond were still tired from travelling and the others just couldn't be bothered to venture out. Even Edison and Caroline made the effort and joined them for dinner, although Johnson cried off saying he wasn't hungry and would stay in his room. The evening passed without incident with great food and flowing conversation and nearly everyone had retired to their rooms by eleven o'clock, apart from Mandy that is who stayed in the bar drinking with a couple of guests she got talking to, until the early hours.

Tuesday 9th September

The next morning saw Andrea and Jack up at the crack of dawn and down to breakfast before any of their group, as they were both excited about seeing their children, even though Jack was a bit disappointed that Luke couldn't be there with them as well. His sunburn wasn't quite as painful as the day before but he had already decided to stay out of the sun for the day to let it heal.

They had eaten breakfast and were round the pool, Andrea sunning herself and Jack under the umbrella, before the rest of them even started getting up. Lizzie and Raymond were the first one's down, closely followed by Elaine and Sid. Edison joined them a few minutes later, excusing Caroline as she had another one of her "heads" and Mandy didn't quite make breakfast at all, showing up instead around eleven thirty, complete with obligatory dark glasses and a floppy hat, proceeding then to sleep under the umbrella for most of the day. As usual, Johnson was nowhere to be seen.

'Do you know what, I haven't even seen your nephew yet' said Elaine as her and Sid joined Andrea and Jack round the pool. 'Are you sure he turned up?'

'Who Johnson?' asked Jack 'Yeh, he's definitely here. He's not one for conversation or having meals with families and he certainly doesn't sunbathe. To be quite honest, I don't know what the hell he came out here for.'

'Most probably frightened of missing out on something' said Andrea, who wasn't a great fan of Johnson. 'Oh and the fact that he didn't have to put his hand in his pocket might have had something to do with it.'

'You didn't pay for him, did you?' asked Elaine.

'No way. If I'd have had my way I wouldn't even have invited him, the little shit. Oh no, Mummy and Daddy pay for everything don't they. I think they're his only source of income at the moment as he lost his last job. In fact I don't think he's ever kept a job more than a few weeks and it's only Edison's influence that gets him employed in the first place. He left his really expensive private school with no qualifications so he couldn't go to university and then after his Dad paid for him to enrol on an accountancy course; he got thrown off it for selling drugs to his classmates. Although we don't mention that in front of Caroline as she thinks he left because the course wasn't up to scratch. She honestly thinks the sun shines out of that boys' arse. I'd love her to find out what an evil little twat he really is.'

'I can tell you've got a lot of time for him Andrea' laughed Sid. 'Now on a brighter note, what time did you say the kids were landing as, believe it or not, it's almost twelve o'clock?'

'Oh my God, they must have already landed then. Jack, pass me over my iPad and I'll check on the arrivals.'

After confirming that their flight had indeed landed, Andrea popped up to her room to quickly freshen up and swapped her sarong for a summery kaftan to put on over her bikini. By the time she came back down, Jack, Elaine and Sid had de-camped to the snack bar area for a bit of shade and had just ordered a round of much needed cold drinks to cool them down. They left Lizzie and Raymond, who were engrossed in their books, and Mandy who was snoring her head off, around the pool area.

'That feels better' said Andrea as she sat down to a very welcoming glass of sparkling water with loads of ice. 'I must admit I was starting to melt over there. I don't mind sitting round the pool but I swear it must be twenty degrees hotter than on the beach.'

'I must admit it does get a bit stifling sometimes' agreed Elaine. 'I don't think it's any hotter, it's just you haven't got that lovely breeze up here that you've got on the beach. Now everyone's here, perhaps we can go to the beach tomorrow.'

'Sounds like a plan Laney. We'll definitely have a whole day on the beach tomorrow. I know Sophie and the boys will be up for it as they love the sea. Talking of which I think that's their taxi just pulled up.'

They quickly finished their drinks and walked over to the reception area where, sure enough, Sophie, Jamie and Stephen were just walking up the steps with their cases. After Andrea and Jack greeted their respective offspring with lots of hugs and kisses, the three new arrivals checked in with Christos and went to their rooms to unpack, promising their parents they would meet them in the snack bar for lunch in about half an hour.

True to their word the three of them arrived at the snack bar just as Lizzie and Raymond had joined the throng and they all ordered lunch.

'Oh my word, I can't believe what a beautiful young lady Sophie has grown into' said Lizzie, who was just getting over the shock of how much like Carlo, her friends daughter looked like. 'She really is a credit to you Andrea.'

'Thanks Lizzie, I must admit I couldn't be any prouder of her if I tried.'

Sophie, with her dark curly hair and olive skin that she inherited from Carlo and her piercing emerald green eyes that she inherited from Andrea, was absolutely stunning. Spending most of her time in jeans and t-shirts with her hair scraped back and no makeup, she really had no idea of how attractive she was.

Although still single, she'd had two previous relationships that were quite serious. The most recent one was with a guy she worked with, which ended just three months ago. Her home, a two bedroomed house, just five minutes' walk from her mum, is shared with her golden retriever and two cats and at the present time she is quite happy being single. She is very close to both her mum and dad and tries to visit Carlo in Italy as often as she can.

Born with her dad's love of food, she went to catering college and then worked in London in a top hotel. After being left some money when Andrea's father died, she took a risk and opened a small Italian restaurant only minutes from where she lives. Simple food, like 'nonna' makes, a great atmosphere and low prices has given Sophie a successful business.

She gets on famously with Jack, as well as being best friends with her, soon to be, stepbrother Jamie and his partner Stephen, and is over the moon that Jack and her mum are getting married.

'Oh shut up Mum, you're embarrassing me' said Sophie in mock mortification, as Andrea continued to sing her praises.'

'You sound like our son Adam' said Raymond. 'He hates it if Lizzie praises him in front of people. Unfortunately, that's what parents do. You wait until you have children of your own Sophie, you'll do exactly the same and then wonder why they cringe with embarrassment.'

'I know Mum means well, but I get so embarrassed when she tells people how well I have done. Even though I've got my own business, I'd never brag about it and I'd hate to think anyone think I was conceited or anything.'

'I'm sure no-one would think that Sophie' said Jack 'unlike my nephew Johnson, who brags about anything and everything. Now that's conceited, or actually in his case pompous would be the better choice of word. Anyway sorry, where are my manners, for those of you who don't know, this is my youngest son Jamie and his partner Stephen. Jamie actually works in the restaurant with Sophie as a trainee chef and at one point we didn't think they would both be able to get over here but they managed to get an agency chef, who they were both comfortable with to cover so, happy days.'

Jamie, Jack's youngest son, who looked a lot younger than his thirty four years, with his boyish good looks, had a mop of highlighted hair and eyelashes most women would pay a fortune for. Openly gay, he lives with Stephen, his partner of just over a year. Stephen who is nearly twelve years older than Jamie, is the calming influence he needed in his life. They both live in a converted warehouse overlooking the Thames, which also doubles up as a gallery for, up and coming artist, Stephen to show his work. Jamie, who works as a trainee chef with Sophie is also studying for his catering diploma at college two days a week and both he and Stephen plan to get married once he has finished college.

Jamie was only four years old when his mother left home, although it didn't affect him greatly as he was too young at the time. The death of Jack's second wife Paula some years later, also didn't affect him much as he was more worried at the time about telling his family that he was gay. Unfortunately at that time both Jack and his older brother Luke were too caught up in their own grief to worry about what Jamie was going through and it resulted in him going off the rails for a while. After a few years of partying hard and sleeping with both men and women, he finally came out to his family when he was twenty four. Jack and Luke both accepted his sexuality and were just upset that he felt he couldn't have confided in them earlier.

Jack's brother Edison was disgusted when he was told and seemed to think it was some sort of psychological illness and he needed therapy and pills to "put him right". Jamie's cousin, Johnson has always treated him like a leper and calls him a "dirty little faggot" whenever he speaks about him. Needless to say he doesn't meet up with that part of the family very often! Jamie adores Andrea, who totally accepted him from day one, and is also inseparable from Sophie, who loves him as the brother she never had. He was really looking forward to the wedding but not so much meeting up with Edison and Johnson again.

'It's great having all the family out here, it's just a shame Luke and Melinda couldn't come over but, at the end of the day, he should be with his wife if she's ill. How is she by the way?'

'Actually Dad, has Luke not called you? I know he said he'd been trying to.'

'I don't know Jamie, my phone's in the safe. Why has something happened?'

'Unbelievable, how is anyone supposed to get hold of you if your phone's locked up? It's not like anyone is going to nick it. It must be about ten years old. Anyway, he's been trying to get hold of you to let you know about Melinda. She got taken into hospital with stomach pains, which Luke said he thought might be appendicitis. Well it wasn't. It turns out she's pregnant and they thought they might have lost the baby. She's just got the all clear but obviously she has to rest up and can't travel. So it looks like you're going to be a grandad, old man.'

'Wow, I think that is definitely a cause for celebration. Congratulations mate.' said Sid as he called over to the bar to order a couple of bottles of champagne to be put on ice and brought over. 'Right bubbly's on its way, so let's order some lunch and get this party started'

107

'Bloody hell, I can't believe I'm going to be a grandad!' said Jack. 'So that means you're going to be a step-granny. Don't worry I'll get you a rocking chair when we get home so you can do your knitting in comfort. Oh and one of those push along trolley's for when you go shopping'

'Oh you are so not funny' said Andrea, looking around for something to throw at Jack. 'Please tell me I don't look old enough to be a grandmother.'

'No Mum, you so don't. I really can't ever see you as a traditional grey haired granny knitting booties. In fact I can't see you as the maternal type at all, even though you did have me so you must have done a pretty good job of it.'

'Well thank you, child of mine. Great praise indeed' said Andrea laughing. 'Ooh look, here comes the champagne and the food.'

They all got stuck into their lunch and finished off the champagne in record time. After Jack had popped back to his room to phone Luke to congratulate him, he came back down and ordered another couple of bottles. They were still sitting at their table drinking Champagne when a voice piped up behind them.

'G'day cobbers. Any of that fizz still going?'

They all turned round to see a handsome, tanned stranger grinning from ear to ear.

'Adam, what the bloody hell are you doing here?' exclaimed Raymond, jumping to his feet to hug his son.

'Lovely welcome that is' laughed Adam. 'Remind me to surprise you more often!'

'You know I didn't mean it like that son, you just shocked me, that's all. I really didn't expect to see you here. I suppose you was in on this?'

'Who me?' said Lizzie, looking shocked. 'Of course I was. We thought it would be a nice surprise for you, seeing as you're sixty tomorrow.'

'Oh no, please don't remind me' groaned Raymond, 'I had just about forgotten about that. But, age aside, it is a wonderful surprise. Right, Adam let me introduce you to everyone here.'

Adam went around the group shaking everyone's hand and once everyone had been suitably introduced, they got back to the champagne and some more food that had been ordered. They then proceeding to sit around drinking, eating and chatting until the sun started to go down.

'So how many people have you got going to the actual wedding then Andrea?' asked Lizzie.

'I think the final number is now twenty two, although that can always change before the day. There's all us lot and then another three couples that we know from coming here every year. In fact, they should be arriving here this evening on the Birmingham flight. They are a really nice bunch of people, you'll love them and we've also invited Spiros who runs the snack place on the beach, and his wife Ria. Then what we've done is put out an open invite to other guests we know and the staff to come to the evening do. Oh and we've also invited George, who owns the restaurant we're going to tomorrow night and his wife, Veronica, to come to the evening do as well.'

'Bloody hell, has anyone seen the time' said Sid pointing to his watch. 'It's nearly seven o'clock and people are starting to come down for their dinner'.

'So what, that's what holidays are all about' said Raymond. 'Doing things on the spur of the moment and just going with the flow. Our lives are regimented enough when we're at work.'

'I make you right mate' said Jack, 'so who wants another drink then?'

They all sat around for a while longer before gradually drifting off to their rooms to shower and change. After drinking most of the afternoon, no-one wanted a heavy night and since they had had a late lunch and lots of nibbles with their champagne no-one was really that hungry. As it was gone eight thirty by the time they all met again in reception, they all decided to just get pizzas in the bar across the road. After eating, the excitement of the day started to take its toll and nearly everyone was back in their rooms and asleep before midnight.

Wednesday 10th September

The next morning saw most of the guests meeting up at breakfast so they could wish Raymond a happy birthday. He and Lizzie, together with Adam, Sophie, Jamie and Stephen then went off to catch the free bus to Vassilikos beach which was around half an hour away. It was there that they all planned to do some water sports, apart from Lizzie that is, who would lay on the beach with a book and watch them. Mandy stayed round the pool, along with Edison and Caroline and Johnson disappeared off somewhere, as usual.

Elaine, Sid, Andrea and Jack all made their way down to the beach in the resort, preferring to spend the day in peace and quiet rather than listening to music blaring out and the sound of jet skis and motor boats revving up. The only water sports that they were interested in, were getting on and off of their airbeds in the sea.

'I thought the kids were coming down the beach with us today' said Elaine as the four friends strolled down the lane to the beach.

'No, they've gone to some beach over the other side of the island where they can do some watersports' said Andrea, 'I think this was a bit quiet for them. They did ask us if we wanted to come but I think my days of dashing about on a jet ski or one of those bananas are long past.'

'Oh you should have said yes Andrea, we could have all had a right laugh' teased Sid. 'I know Elaine likes nothing better than to be thrown off an inflatable that's going through the water at eighty miles per hour!'

'Well, we can always turn round and go back there if you want' laughed Andrea, stopping in the road.

'No, you're alright babe, I think we'll stick to sunbathing' said Elaine looking horrified at the thought of getting on anything faster than a pedalo.

'I didn't see Mark and Paula and the others this morning, did you?' asked Jack, 'I assume their plane got in alright last night.'

'Yeh, it did. Sorry, I meant to tell you' said Sid, 'I saw Mark with Doug and Keith this morning when I popped down to get some milk for my tea. They were just going off for a walk and the girls were still in their pits. I said we'd see them in the bar tonight to confirm details of the wedding times.'

'No problem mate, I just wanted to make sure they'd got here OK. It'll be nice to see them all again though. Can't believe it's been a year since we last saw them.'

'I know, where does the time go to?' agreed Elaine, 'this holiday's racing on as well. Before we know it, we'll be back home in the rain and cold, looking forward to Christmas.'

'Right, that's quite enough of that Laney' said Sid, 'you know we don't use the 'C' word until at least November and we've still got plenty of time left before we have to go home. Now give me some Euros, we're nearly at the shop.'

After stopping off to buy the obligatory bottled water and newspaper, they picked out four sun beds nearest to the shoreline and laid their towels out. Within an hour or so of settling down, Sid started to get a bit restless and managed to talk the others into taking a walk up the beach to the next resort. After waiting for the girls to put on sarongs and put their beach bags under the sun beds, taking with the just their phones and purses, they set off down the beach.

'I can't believe you bullied us into walking all this way' moaned Elaine and Andrea, who were getting slower and slower, the further along the beach they went. 'We were quite happy laying on the sun beds.'

'No-one forced you into coming. You only tagged along because you thought you might miss something so if you're going to moan about it, you might as well go back and me and Jack will go off on our own.'

'Well, we're halfway along now so we might as well carry on' said Elaine picking up the pace a bit, 'and to be fair, I wouldn't mind a drink or two in that nice bar at the end of the beach.'

'Oh I know the one you mean' said Andrea, trying to keep up with her friend, 'isn't it called Serenity or something?'

'Yep, that's the one. I've seen pictures of it on Facebook, it looks really lovely. It's got great big cushions to sit on the beach and the cocktails look amazing. I think they do food as well so we could have a bit of lunch while we're there!'

'Oh that's great, that is. We decide to have a walk along the beach and, before you know it, these two have planned the rest of the day for us.'

'Sid, you just knew that would happen though, didn't you?' laughed Jack. 'I think it's just best we go with the flow for an easy life. But I do think, as going to this bar is the girl's idea, then they should pay for lunch.'

'Too right mate. I'm not proud; I'll accept a free lunch from anyone.'

'Good job I brought my purse along with me then, wasn't it?' said Elaine, 'otherwise you would have had to have paid for it.'

'Actually, I've just thought, I'll be paying for it anyway. All the money we've got with us, I got out of my account.'

'Yes but it's in my purse and possession is nine tenths of the law, isn't that what they say?'

'Cheeky mare. See what I have to put up with Jack. Are you sure you want to get married? It's not all it's cracked up to be.'

'Whoa, you're skating on thin ice there mate. I think they both might be ganging up on you if you're not careful.'

'Oh look, isn't this the bar we want' said Sid, changing the subject quickly as the girls had just scooped up a handful of sand to throw at him.

'Okay, you got out of it this time' said Elaine emptying the sand from her hands, 'we don't want to cover the place in sand. But don't forget we have to walk back.'

They all brushed the sand off their feet and walked into the bar to find a table. Although there were big cushions that were dotted around that you could either sit on the terrace with or take down to the beach, they all decided that more than a few minutes on them would cause havoc with their backs. Instead they sat inside on big comfy chairs in the cool.

They all ordered the Serenity Special which was a vodka based cocktail that came complete with a small fruit and veg shop. Both Elaine and Andrea took some photos of each other with the drinks to put on Facebook and after cooling down and quenching their thirst, they ordered some lunch. As it was Raymond's sixtieth birthday bash at The Sunset Grill that evening and they didn't want to spoil their appetite, they just ordered a large plate of nachos to share, which were more than enough for them as the portion sizes were huge. The bar was really chilled, playing some fabulous old school eighties music and they agreed that it was definitely somewhere that they would like to come back to. Elaine wasted no time in uploading pictures of the food and surroundings onto her food site, letting everyone on there know what a great place it was.

'It's really nice in here, isn't it?' said Elaine, tucking into her nachos 'I love the music. I bet it's really good here at night. I've seen pictures of it on Facebook, it's all lit up with strings of fairy lights.'

'Oh well, you two would be right at home then' laughed Jack.

'Oh ha, ha, very funny. There's nothing wrong with having a few lights to brighten the place up.'

'No, there's not' admitted Jack, 'but you two do go a bit overboard though. I reckon the National Grid breathes a sign of relief when you go on holiday. You're the only people I know who take fairy lights on holiday with them.'

'You're just jealous Jack, but we have got some spare ones if you want to do your balcony up.'

'No, you're alright Laney; I think I'll live without them.'

'Suit yourself, don't say I didn't offer. Now is anyone having some coffees before we have to do that hike back?'

After having their coffee and buying a couple of bottles of water for the return journey, they paid the bill and started the walk along the beach to where their sun beds were. By the time they got back they were knackered so, after a quick swim, they all got under their umbrellas and had a couple of hours sleep.

They all woke up around the same time and all four of them went in the sea for the last swim of the day before coming back to lie in the sun to dry off.

'Oh, this is the life' sighed Elaine, stretching out on her sun bed.

'Living the dream babes' said Sid.

'Yeh, chicken or beef!'

'Chicken or beef? What the hell is that about?' asked Jack, looking completely bemused.

'Oh, we always say that if someone mentions "living the dream". The daughter of one of our friends got a job as an Air Stewardess and one day when we was asking her how she was enjoying her job, Sid said that she must be living the dream and she replied, 'Oh yes, chicken or beef'. We thought it was hilarious, especially since you wouldn't expect that from the airline that she works for as it's more of a "steak or lobster" outfit.'

'OK' said Jack, 'but I still don't understand the chicken or beef bit.'

'You're not the sharpest tool in the box sometimes are you' laughed Elaine. 'Think back to when you used to get a meal on the plane. The stewardess used to come round and ask everyone what they wanted and it was always chicken or beef.'

'Oh my God, you're right' said Jack, the penny finally dropping, 'they did, didn't they. I do miss the old airline meals, as bad as they were. It was part of your holiday. There's loads of stuff you don't get anymore. The little bags of peanuts with your drinks, hot towels after your meal and pillows and blankets. You don't even get anything on the telly on most short haul flight now. It's not right.'

'It's the way of the world now mate, I'm afraid. You seem to pay more and get less' said Sid.

After drying off, they got their stuff together and Andrea, Jack and Elaine headed back to the hotel to start getting ready for that evening's meal, while Sid quickly walked up to the Sunset Grill to drop off a bag of table confetti, balloons and banners that Elaine had bought when they were in Zante Town to decorate the table with.

Lizzie had arranged a meet up in the bar at seven o'clock that evening as she had arranged glasses of bubbly and some nibbles as a pre-dinner birthday drink for Raymond. As the table at the Sunset Grill had been booked for eight thirty, they had plenty of time for a couple of drinks and to be able to mingle before they started the walk up to the end of the resort where the restaurant was.

Andrea and Jack got down to the bar a few minutes before everyone else so they could see their friends from Birmingham, get them a drink and fill them in with the details for the wedding on Friday. Once Elaine and Sid joined them, they all chatted about what they had been doing through the year, before joining Lizzie, Raymond and the rest of their family and friends.

Everyone in their party had turned up pretty much on time, some making more of an effort than others. Caroline and Edison waltzed in done up to the nines as usual and Johnson finally turned up just as everyone was getting ready to leave.

'Oh look what the cat dragged in' said Jack to Johnson as he sauntered through reception to the waiting party. 'I thought it was just a rumour that you were here, seeing as you haven't said one word to anyone since you arrived.'

'Yes, nice to see you too Uncle Jackson' said Johnson, with his face set in a permanent sneer. 'I see my favourite cousin is here then, and still hasn't outgrown his 'gay' phase. I still can't believe you put up with it. If he was my brother, father would have beaten it out of him by now.'

'Well it's a good job I'm Jamie's dad then isn't it, because I'm not a bigoted, homophobe like my brother and I'll tell you something else, son' Jack pulled Johnson to one side so he wasn't overheard. 'If I catch you slagging off my son or his partner to anyone again, I might just have to let mummy dearest know what a snivelling, drug taking, bully her darling son really is. That's after I knock your teeth down your throat.'

'Oh very grown up. You don't know anything about me and exactly who do you think mother is going to believe; the son she dotes on, or her low-class brother-in-law who she looks down on. I'm so very scared!'

'Just keep it up fat boy and you'll find out what being scared is really about. Now you keep out of my way and I'll keep out of yours, fair enough.'

Johnson pushed past Jack and walked back over to his parents, still smirking.

'Honestly, one of these days I'll knock that smirk right off of that ugly mug of his' said Jack to Andrea as they started the walk down to the restaurant.

'I think you may find there is a queue for that' she laughed. 'Now forget Johnson and let's look forward to a lovely evening. So what are you having to eat tonight then Laney?'

They all took a slow walk to The Sunset Grill, arriving there just before half past eight. The place was packed to the rafters but no sooner had they got through the door than the owner, George Liasades, came over to greet them. He showed them all to a large table that had been bedecked with the balloons, banners and table confetti, that Sid had dropped off earlier, as well as ice buckets full of bubbly that George had laid on.

'Oh George, you really have done us proud mate, this looks amazing' said Jack as they were seated.

'My pleasure Jack. Now who's the birthday boy?'

Introductions were made to George and to Tassos, the waiter that would be looking after them that evening. Menus were handed round whilst glasses of chilled bubbly were poured out for everyone.

Raymond clinked his glass with a fork to get everyone's attention.

'Sorry, won't keep you a minute, I just wanted to thank everyone for coming tonight and for putting all this on. I really appreciate it guys and I think this will definitely be an evening to remember.'

Everyone raised their glasses and toasted Raymond's good health before turning their attention back to the menus.

It wasn't long before plate after plate of food was being brought up to the hungry guests. Greek specials such as Moussaka, Pasticio and Kleftico were served along with steak, chicken and fresh fish that had been barbecued to order, all accompanied by bowls of Greek salad, chips and pitta bread.

Even a pizza was served to a petulant Johnson who complained about eating all this foreign muck! Everybody tucked in and made light work of the food. In fact there wasn't a plate on the table that wasn't cleared, even Mandy managed to work her way through a plain grilled chicken fillet and some chips.

Elaine was in her element, taking photos with her iPad of every dish that was brought up.

'My dear, why do you keep taking pictures of everyone's food?' asked Caroline after Elaine snapped her massive plate of fillet steak and all the trimmings.

'Oh take no notice of her Caroline' said Sid, 'she's got a food site on Facebook that she runs so we're used to her taking photos of everything we eat and drink out here.'

'Really, why on earth would you want to put pictures of food and drink on the internet? Surely people can just come and sample the dishes themselves or am I being a little old fashioned.'

'Yeh I think perhaps you maybe Caroline.' said Jack, 'Unfortunately everyone lives their life on Facebook nowadays and most people want to see what they're getting before they go. It's the way of the world now, whether you love it or hate it.'

'Well I think I'll give it a miss thank you. I've never been on this Facebook thing and I honestly couldn't think of anything worse than looking at pictures of what people have been eating. It's all very strange if you ask me.'

Elaine and Andrea looked at each other, both trying desperately not to laugh as Jack changed the subject quickly asking who wanted coffees.

Coffees and liqueurs were brought up, not long after desserts had been served to the few that had room and by now the restaurant had started to empty out with only a couple of tables, apart from theirs, still occupied. George came over and sat with the party, informing them that his wife had just called so say she was now leaving her shop to join them all for a drink or two. Tassos came over and asked what everyone wanted for a drink on the house and by the time he had brought them out and handed everyone a drink, Veronica was pulling up outside the restaurant in her car.

George noticed and went outside to meet her so he could introduce her to everyone.

'Oh look here comes George's wife, Veronica. She made it after all' said Andrea waving to her as she made her way through the restaurant.

'How do you know her then?' asked Sid.

'I went in her shop to get a few bits when me and Jack popped into Zante town the other day. She's really nice actually. I was hoping she would turn up because she's Australian and comes from Melbourne where Raymond and Lizzie live. Not that they would know her or anything, it's not that small a world!'

'I wouldn't be so sure of that' said Jack, staring at the approaching Veronica.

'What do you mean babe?' asked Andrea, 'Are you OK, only you've gone as white as a sheet'

'Yeh I think so, it's just Veronica, she looks just like…, no it can't be.'

'Can't be who?'

'Well, I know it's silly but George's wife is the spitting image of my first wife, Diane. Surely she couldn't be, could she?'

Jack didn't have to wait long for an answer to his question. George introduced his wife to everyone but as he got to Jack, Veronica stood in front of him in total shock.

'Oh my God, Jack. What the hell are you doing here?'

'Hello Diane' said Jack bitterly. 'I could ask you the same really. I thought I recognised you when you walked in but I was hoping it was just someone who looked like you. No such luck, eh?'

'Jack?' asked Andrea, 'Are you sure? Is Veronica actually your first wife?'

'Yeh unfortunately she is babe. Sorry, I'm forgetting my manners, everyone this is Diane Blake my first wife who walked out on me and my boys thirty years ago, leaving me in debt and having to pick up the pieces when our sons were falling apart after losing their mum.'

Veronica, or Diane as she was actually called, stood routed to the spot, unable to speak.

'Is this true?' cried Jamie as he got up from his seat. 'Are you really my mum?'

'Oh Jamie' cried Diane, 'I can't believe you're here as well. This is turning into a nightmare. I never meant to hurt any of you, I only meant to go away for a while to get my head together and then I was going to come back. But things got on top of me and the longer I stayed away, the harder it was to come back. You know how things get'

'No, not really Diane' said Jack, going over to his son who was obviously very distressed. 'Things have never got that bad that I felt I had to leave my family then empty the bank account, oh and the fraudulently take out a second mortgage on the strength of your sons' inheritance. Don't try and make out you were the victim here. You were and always will be an evil, self-centred bitch and even now when you've been caught out, you're still spewing lies. I bet George doesn't know what a conniving, lying cow he has married, does he?'

'No he doesn't' agreed George, looking like his whole world had just caved in. 'Is this true Veronica? Did you walk out on Jack and your sons? Because if it is, and you have been living a lie for the whole time you have been married to me, then I really don't think I can cope with that. You told me that you had no children and that your last husband had died, that's why you came to Zante, to get over it. How could you lie about that? Is there anything else you haven't told me or is your whole life and our marriage a sham?'

'No, there's nothing else, I swear. Living with you has been the happiest time of my life and I swear I haven't lied about anything since we've been married.'

'Ah, but how can I believe anything you say now Veronica. Or should I call you Diane. I think perhaps it's best that you leave the restaurant now. We will talk more about this when I get home; I have customers to see to.'

George looked at his wife as if he were seeing her for the first time, then turned and walked away from her.

131

Before she left, Veronica turned and looked at Jamie who had been listening to everything that had been said.

'Oh Jamie, my baby boy. Look at you; I can't believe what a handsome young man you've grown into. Where's erm, my other boy?'

'Your other boy' spat Jamie, looking at his mother in disgust, 'you can't even remember his name can you? Luke, had to stay in the UK as his wife has just found out she's having a baby and had some complications. But I don't really know why I'm telling you this as he would never let you within a mile of his baby. You're hardly grandmother material are you? Luke took it badly when you left and in his eyes you're dead and, you know what, you are to me as well. Andrea here has been more of a mother to me than you ever were so why don't you do us all a favour and crawl back under that rock you came from.'

Veronica went to walk over to where Jamie was standing but Jack stopped her.

'Jamie's right, he's got all the family he could ever want right here so why don't you just do everyone a favour and leave before someone does something they might regret.'

Veronica took one last look at Jamie and, eyes welling up; she turned and ran out of the restaurant to her car, as George came back over to the table, looking distraught.

'Oh Jack, I am so sorry for this. I swear I never knew my wife had such history. Believe me; if I had known her whole life was a pack of lies, I would never have married her.'

'George, none of this is your fault. There's no way you could have known that your wife was my ex, so please don't blame yourself. I just hope you can work your way through this. I got over her walking out on me years ago; it's doing what she did to my boys that I'll never forgive her for. But hey, if it hadn't happened then I wouldn't have met Andrea or half the people sitting round this table. In fact I most probably would never have even set foot on this island, so I do have that to thank her for. Now let us have the bill and we'll settle up and let you get home, I think it may be a long night for you!'

When the bill came up they split it between them, adding in Raymond and Lizzie's share so they didn't have to pay, and settled up, leaving a generous tip for Tassos. After saying their goodbyes and thanking George for a great, if not eventful evening, everyone made their way back to the hotel.

Jack and Andrea caught up with Jamie and Stephen who were trying to keep some distance between themselves and Johnson.

'Are you alright son' asked Jack, concerned for his youngest and what he had just witnessed.

'I'm fine dad, honestly. I got over not having a mum years ago and seeing her now, well I didn't feel a thing. As I said, Andrea has been more of a mother to me than that woman ever could be. I think the best thing we can do now is forget she ever existed, put this behind us and concentrate on having the best holiday and wedding ever.'

'Do you know what, I think that's the most sensible thing I've ever heard you say Jamie' said Jack giving his son a hug. 'Now, before I start getting all emotional, who's coming to the bar for a nightcap?

134

My treat, as an apology for interrupting Raymond's birthday meal.'

'You don't have to apologise Jack' said Raymond, 'how on earth could you possibly have guessed that after thirty years, your ex-wife would suddenly turn up in a taverna in Greece. Honestly mate, you couldn't write it, could you?'

'No, I suppose you couldn't. As long as it didn't spoil your birthday meal.'

'You're kidding mate. I haven't had this much fun in ages. Now where's this drink, as they say in Oz, "I'm as dry as a dead dingo's donger"!'

Thursday 11th September

The day before the wedding saw most of the party down at breakfast quite early and all looking remarkably refreshed, considering the events of the previous evening.

Whilst having a nightcap in the bar when they returned, Petros had managed to sell Jack tickets for them all to go to the hotels' weekly barbeque night. Both Andrea and Jack had thought it would be a good idea to use it as a pre-wedding get together as neither of them were really up for the traditional stag and hen parties that Mandy was trying to organise for them.

'I'm really looking forward to the barbecue tonight. Thanks again for getting the tickets Jack, are you sure you don't want any money for them? ' said Lizzie, as she and Raymond sat down at the table next to Andrea and Jack.

'No, definitely not. It's mine and Andrea's treat for everyone. It will be good to let our hair down and have a bit of a dance. The entertainment's normally quite good at these evenings and to be honest I'd much prefer to do this than go on a bar crawl and get absolutely plastered, like Mandy wanted us to do.'

'Yeh, I think we may all be a little long in the tooth for all that now.'

'You speak for yourself love' laughed Sid. 'I'm quite capable of doing a bar crawl with the rest of the kids out there.'

'Course you are Sid' said Elaine, rolling her eyes up to heaven. 'Last time you had a skin full, you had to have the next day off work as you felt so rough. I think Lizzie is right, we are all a little too old for boozing all night and I for one am really looking forward to the barbecue night.'

After breakfast, everyone went their separate ways, some to the beach, some round the pool and Johnson, who knows where! Andrea and Jack had to go over a few things for the wedding with Anita, so Elaine and Sid said they would meet them at the beach later on that morning.

They took a leisurely walk down to the beach and once they had ordered lunches from Spiro to be picked up later, they managed to get their normal sun beds, paying for both theirs and Andreas and Jacks. As they were going out that evening, they decided to just chill out on the beach all day, topping up their tans. Andrea and Jack joined them at around eleven thirty along with an adorable little white dog that had followed them all the way from the hotel.

'Oh look at him, he's gorgeous' said Elaine as Andrea and Jack plonked themselves down on the sun beds that had been saved for them, 'has he got a name tag on his collar?'

'No, I looked for one earlier but at least he has got a collar on so he must belong to someone.'

'Not necessarily' said Elaine as she made a fuss of the little dog, 'the volunteers that look after the strays try to get collars on them because people are less likely to poison or shoot them as they can't be sure that they don't belong to someone.'

'Oh God, that's awful, why would you want to hurt an adorable little thing like this? I honestly think some people are sick.'

They all made a fuss of the dog, who finally went to sleep under Elaine's sun lounger. The others then followed suit and dozed off until Sid's watch beeped, letting them know it was one o'clock and time to pick up their lunch from Spiro.

'Right' said Sid. Jumping up and grabbing his wallet from out of his bag. 'I've ordered a selection of baguettes and got Spiro to cut each one into four so we can have a bit of each, hope that's alright for everyone. Now what do you all want to drink?'

After getting everyone's drinks order, Sid started to walk up the beach to get the lunch.

'Actually Sid, hold on I think I'd better come with you' shouted Elaine after him. 'Last time you went and got the lunch you were gone ages and we're all bloody starving.'

With Elaine hot on his heels, Sid got to Spiro's van and picked up the baguettes, adding in two cans of fizzy orange and a couple of coffees. Elaine then picked out a large bag of crisps and a doughnut to share with Andrea.

'Well, it's going to be a long night tonight' said Elaine, noticing the look Sid gave her, 'and we need to line our stomachs.'

'Blimey, yours will be so lined you won't have any room for the alcohol if you're not careful.'

'Oh very funny. Now pay the man and let's get back on that beach before I waste away.'

They both made their way back to the others with the bag of food to find Andrea and Jack falling over themselves laughing.

'Flipping hell, we've only been gone ten minutes and they've lost the plot' said Elaine putting their lunch down on the sun bed. 'Right, what's tickled you two?'

'I was just telling Jack about the time Mandy got the window cleaner's name wrong. Do you remember, when she was staying at mine that time?'

'Oh God yes I do' said Andrea starting to laugh. 'I didn't think she would ever live that down'

'Right, go on then, let me in on it' said Sid.

'I told you about it ages ago, but knowing you it went in one ear and out the other'

'I'm sure Elaine told you Sid, it was when Mandy was staying with me and Sophie while she was having some work done on her flat. I asked her if she could pay the window cleaner for me while I was out and when I got in she told me that she'd written him a cheque so I thought no more of it. Anyway, that evening the doorbell goes and there's the window cleaner standing there with the cheque that Mandy had written him in his hand. He didn't look very happy and asked me if I thought I was having a laugh or something. I didn't have a clue what he was going on about until I saw the cheque. Mandy had only written it out to a Mr Bit'

'No way' laughed Sid, 'what, as in "you've missed a bit"?'

'Yeh, the same. Anyway, I called her out to see the window cleaner and asked her why she had written it and she said, completely straight faced, that she had been out front when he was cleaning a neighbours windows and heard someone shout out "oy, missed a bit" and just assume that his name was Mr Bit. Luckily the window cleaner also found it hilarious and use to rib her about it every time he came round.'

'Oh honestly, only Mandy could think something like that' said Sid, wiping his eyes, 'that's made my day, that has. Now get those baguettes out I've worked up a bit of an appetite now.'

'Why have I got a chunk of my baguette missing?' asked Jack holding up his decapitated lunch for them to see.

'Actually, so have I' said Sid, 'what's going on?'

'Ah, I didn't think you'd notice' said Elaine looking guilty, 'I thought I take a bit off the end to give to Charlie.'

'Who the bloody hell is Charlie?' said Sid looking around for the offending person.

'Charlie, the dog' said Elaine pointing to the little dog who was now happily chomping on Jack and Sid's baguettes.

'How do you know he's called Charlie?'

'I don't. I just thought he looked like a Charlie'

'He's not the only one that looks like a right Charlie' laughed Sid, 'Me and Jack have to make do with half our lunch while old Charlie boy here is munching away without a care in the world. Anyway, why are we feeding him when, if I remember rightly, we had to pay a small fortune in excess baggage fees because of all the dog treats you brought out? Why is he not eating those instead of my lunch?'

'Oh bugger, I forgot about those, they're all still in my suitcase. Remind me when we get back to pop out and drop them into the shop at the top of the road. They have a pick up every day to take to the strays. I can't believe I forgot about them. Honestly, I'd forget my head if it wasn't screwed on.'

They spent the next half an hour or so eating what was left of their lunch after Charlie had had his fill, before getting into the shade for the now obligatory after lunch snooze. Once their food had gone down, they spent the rest of the afternoon in and out of the sea, and generally larking about, before drying off and taking a slow walk back to the hotel to get ready for the evening. Charlie didn't follow them back as he had found another couple to sit with who just happened to have opened a large bag of crisps.

The barbecue night that was held around the pool, started at seven thirty with the food being served at around eight thirty. Tables were all set out as per the table plan that was placed by the bar. Jack's party of fourteen were seated at one large table and everyone started moving over to be seated after having a quick drink the bar beforehand. There was Greek music playing in the background while everyone ate and later on there would be some Greek dancers and then a DJ playing until late. Everyone was looking forward to the evening and the atmosphere was buzzing, even Johnson seemed animated.

With the first of the meat starting to go on the barbecue, there was soon a wonderful smell wafting over to all of the tables and everybody was chomping at the bit to get called up for their food. The tables were called up one by one and plates were filled with barbecued chicken, pork kebabs, steak and village sausages. There was also a table laden with assorted salads, bread and cheese pastries that everyone could help themselves to.

Once everyone had filled their plates with food, the waiting staff came around with jugs of village wine and beer that were put on all the tables.

'Blimey, this ain't bad is it?' said Sid, pouring himself and Elaine a glass of red. 'I didn't realise you got wine and beer thrown in as well.'

'No, I must admit I didn't even look at the ticket' said Jack, feeling a bit foolish. 'I just thought the price included your dinner and some entertainment. Bit of a result then and it's not bad wine either.'

'No the foods pretty good as well' agreed Andrea, 'in fact I think Elaine's up there now getting some more. Talk of the devil, here she comes.'

'I've just been up to get a bit more salad' said Elaine coming back and plonking herself down, 'and stood behind the two most greedy people I think I have ever seen. You should have seen them piling on the grub. Honestly, you'd think they hadn't eaten in a month. Talk about getting your monies worth!'

'If that's the couple in their early sixties that look as though they are going rambling, then they come here every year.' said Jack.

'Yeh, they did look like they were on a hike actually, all khaki shorts and sensible shoes.'

'That's the ones. You should see them at breakfast. They're normally the first through the door at seven thirty and you've never seen anything like it. They pile it on. A complete full English, half a loaf of toast, pancakes, doughnuts, fruits, yoghurts and cereal. I honestly don't know where they put it. Me and Andrea call them the Greedies!.

'Talking of greedies, how many plates of food have you had now Elaine?'

'This is only my second, and it is only salad. Although I did see them putting out the desserts and I think I may have to go up there and try something.'

'Absolutely' said Andrea 'it would be rude not too and you'd hate to see all that food go to waste.'

After everyone had finished eating, a few of them ordered some coffees and liqueurs and settled down to watch the Greek dancing. Towards the end the dancers got everyone up to join in, apart from Johnson who sat at the table scowling. Even Caroline and Edison managed a few minutes of dancing before sitting back down to keep their son company.

Once the Greek dancing had finished and everything had been cleared away, a DJ started playing songs from the sixties through to present time, complete with the obligatory silly party songs that got everyone going. By about ten o'clock most people were up dancing, although some stayed sitting at their tables as being the worse for wear after overdoing the village red, they could barely stand, let alone dance.

'Right, I don't know about you Lanie but if I don't get to the loo soon, there's going to be an accident' said Andrea after a particularly energetic 'oops upside your head, 'I'm getting too old for all this, my bladder really can't cope anymore.'

'Oh good, I thought it was just me' laughed Elaine, 'I'm standing here crossing my legs. I think all that wine has just decided to make an exit. I could also do with touching up my make-up as well; the sweat's pouring off me'.

'Oh, far too much information ladies' said Sid, cringing, 'right whilst you go off to the ladies, we'll get some drinks. Meet you back at the table.'

Sid and Jack went up to the bar to get a round in while the girls traipsed off to the loo.

When they got back from the ladies Sid and Jack were already sitting down at their table with the drinks, laughing their heads off.

'What's tickled you two then?'

'OMG, you should see Eddie giving it what for over there' laughed Sid, as he handed out the drinks. 'I think Mandy's been plying him with vodka all night and he's like a man possessed. So far we've seen him playing an imaginary fiddle all the way through "Come on Eileen" and then he took off running around the swimming pool to that Proclaimers song about walking five hundred miles. Honestly, I haven't laughed so much for years.'

'Sid's right' agreed Jack, wiping his eyes where he had been laughing so much. 'Everyone's in stitches up by the pool, apart from Caroline that is. She looks like she could kill him, and probably will when she gets him back in the room!'

'Oh I wish I'd seen that' said Andrea, 'I don't think I've ever seen my future brother-in-law drunk or dance for that matter.'

'Well, I've never seen him drunk and he's my brother.' Laughed Jack.

'It is lovely though, watching everyone letting their hair down and having a good time. Plus, they all seem to be getting on really well, which is always a bonus. Lizzie's boy has really hit it off with my Sophie, which is nice as well. Talking of which, have you seen her and Raymond recently?'

'Yeh, I saw them earlier' said Elaine, 'they had just been for a walk. In fact there they are now on the dance floor having a slow dance.'

'Which is what I think we should be doing Sid. Come on; let's have a couple of dances before we hit the sack.'

Reluctantly, Sid and Jack led their ladies onto the dance floor just as Andrea's favourite Michael Buble song came on. After two or three more slow dances, the DJ livened it up a bit by playing some rock and roll, by which time both Andrea and Elaine had had enough for one evening.

'Right, I don't want to be a party pooper but I'm going to call it a night. Some of us are getting married in the morning and I really don't want to be walking down the aisle with bags under my eyes.'

'No you're right Andrea; I think it's time we went up as well. Come on Sid, I'm not having you moaning you've got a hangover tomorrow. Let's say our goodbyes and make our way to bed.'

It took them a further half an hour to say their goodbyes to everyone, fending off everyone's offer of "one for the road", and finally managing to hit the sack at around midnight.

Friday 12th September – The Wedding

The day of the wedding dawned as perfect a day as any bride could wish. There wasn't a cloud in the sky but there was a slight breeze which kept the temperature bearable and not too humid, which was perfect weather for dressing up in wedding regalia.

Both Andrea and Jack were up early and were sat on their balcony having a cuppa when there was a knock on the door.

'It's a good job we're up' said Jack, going over to find out who wanted them that early in the morning, 'I'd have been well pee'd off if we'd decided to have a lie in.'

'It's okay, we saw you sitting on the balcony so we knew you were up' said Elaine as she came bounding into their room with Sid following closely behind.

'Hello you two' said Andrea as she came in from the balcony, 'I see you're up early as well then.'

'We're far too excited to sleep and we wanted to see you before everyone else was up and about to give you this.'

Elaine handed Andrea an envelope.

'What' this then?'

'Well open it and find out.'

Andrea opened the envelope to find a sheet of paper with the Panorama Hotel logo on it.

'It looks like a reservation confirmation for that hotel in Zante Town.'

'We've booked for you to stay there tonight and tomorrow night as a little wedding treat from us and a chance to spend some time on your own as newly-weds.'

'Oh my God, that's amazing. Thank you so much.'

Andrea gave Elaine and Sid and big hug to thank them, wiping her eyes as she got a bit emotional.

'Now you know why we wanted to see you this morning. I knew you'd do this and didn't want you to ruin your wedding make up. I just hope you'll enjoy it.'

'We will Laney, it's perfect. It's really naughty of you though, even though we've always said we fancied staying there' said Jack, also hugging Elaine and Sid.

'I know, that's what made us think of it' said Sid 'Now who fancies an early breakfast seeing as we're up. I don't know about you lot but I'm starving.'

'I'm not sure I could eat anything, my stomach is doing somersaults at the minute' said Andrea, who was definitely looking at bit peaky.

'That's just nerves babe. I know you want everything to go smoothly today and I have no doubt that it will but you do really need to eat something. I don't want my bride to be collapsing at the altar.'

'No, you're right Jack I do need to try and get something down me, even if it's just a slice of toast. We've got a lot to get through today and I'm just so worried that something is going to go wrong.'

'Nothing is going to go wrong Andrea' said Elaine steering her out the door. 'Petros and Anita have got everything organised like a military exercise. Trust me, just enjoy the day and go with the flow. You can't repeat it and you'll kick yourself if you miss the experience because you were worrying too much.'

'Okay,okay! I know when I'm beat. I'll try and relax a bit but I will still be keeping an eye on everything today.'

'We wouldn't expect you to do any different, but you're not going anywhere until we've all had some breakfast.'

The breakfast room was quite busy considering it was still early. The "greedies" were up at the buffet, loading up just as Andrea and Jack had said they did, and most of the wedding party were sitting out by the pool, apart from Edison, who was nursing the hangover from hell, Caroline who had yet another one of her heads and Johnson, who never turned up for breakfast anyway.

Sophie had arranged for a table to accommodate them all and had decorated it with balloons and table confetti. There were also bottles of bubbly chilling, along with jugs of fresh orange juice so everyone could make Bucks Fizz.

'Oh this is lovely' cried Andrea, 'no wonder you two wanted me to come to breakfast so badly.'

'We're just the messengers' said Sid, 'Sophie arranged all this for you, we just had to get you down here at the right time.'

'Right Mum, come and have some Bucks Fizz and something to eat, it might chill you out a little bit. You look like a nervous wreck at the minute. You're getting married, not being executed.'

'I know Sophie, I've just had the third degree off these two. You know what I'm like. I just want everything to go to plan.'

'And it will. I've already seen Petros and Anita and the preparations are in full swing, so you really don't have anything to worry about.'

Andrea took a glass of Bucks Fizz and a croissant from Sophie and after a few minutes she started to relax.

'So, what's everyone going to be doing today then?' asked Sophie

'Well, we've got to go out for a while but we'll have a couple of hours by the pool first' said Elaine.

'Where are you two off to then?' asked Andrea, visibly panicking, 'I thought you were going to help me get ready'

'Don't worry; we'll be back in plenty of time to get you ready'

'Oh good, but you still haven't told me where you're going'

'Just into town, nothing for you to worry about. Some things are just best left alone missy! Right pass me those croissants before Sid eats the bleeding lot.'

After a leisurely breakfast, Elaine and Sid sat round the pool for a while, reading and chatting to the others before booking a taxi and going up to their room to change.

'Right we're off into town now, our taxi should be here any minute' said Elaine, walking back round to the pool area where Andrea and Jack were just getting their stuff together. 'Now is there anything at all you need Andrea?'

'No, I'm sure we're OK hun. If we haven't got everything we need now, we never will have. You two have a good time and we'll see you later. We're just going over to the wedding pavilion to make sure everything is going to plan and see if they need another pair of hands.'

'You should be chilling out today, not running around doing jobs.'

'Actually, I'd rather be doing something otherwise I'll just start worrying that something is going to go wrong. You know what I'm like!'

'I should do by now shouldn't I? Right, we'll see you later.'

Elaine and Sid jumped in the taxi that was waiting for them outside the hotel and set off on the ten minute journey into Zante Town. After paying the driver, they walked over to the Hotel Panorama that they had booked for Andrea and Jack to stay in after the wedding. Andrea explained to the receptionist that the honeymoon suite was booked for their friends and that she had previously spoken to the manager who had said it would be okay for them to come in on the day to decorate the room.

She also paid for the champagne and chocolates that both she and Mandy had ordered to be in the room when the newlyweds arrived.

The receptionist gave them the key and they got in the lift to the top floor where the honeymoon suite was situated. The room was enormous and beautifully decorated. It also came complete with a four poster bed and whirlpool bath and the large balcony afforded them views over Zante Town that were breath-taking.

'Wow, this is amazing' said Elaine walking over to the patio doors and throwing them open. 'Look at those views. I wouldn't mind staying here myself.'

'It is lovely' agreed Sid. 'Perhaps we can come out a bit earlier next year and stay here for a couple of nights before we go to the Ionian Dream.'

'Oh, that would be brilliant. I do hope Andrea and Jack will like it here.'

'To be fair, what's not to like. I think they were well chuffed when we gave them the surprise as it gives them a couple of days on their own before coming back to the mad house. Right now where's all the stuff we bought to decorate this room.'

Elaine produced some silky rose petals that they sprinkled over the bed and some banners and balloons that they dotted around the room, taking care not to damage the walls. After giving it a final once over they left the room and went downstairs to hand the key back in.

'We might as well have a spot of lunch while we're here. We'll need something to keep us going until the wedding reception and at least we'll know that the food's okay for Andrea and Jack.'

'Good thinking Sid. You go and get us a table while I nip to reception and hand the key in'.

Sid managed to get them a table by the window, overlooking the harbour and they both ordered the special of the day, Lamb Panorama, which came in an earthenware pot and was smothered in a thick red wine gravy and sat on a bed of caramelised onions and sliced potatoes. It came with a basket of warm crusty bread for them to mop up the delicious juices and a small carafe of red wine to wash it all down with.

'Blimey, I have to say that's one of the best meals I've had for a long time' said Sid, cleaning the bottom of his dish with the last piece of bread. 'Now, I don't know about you girl, but I'm having a pudding.'

'Yeh, sod it, you only live once, hand over that menu.'

They both ordered the homemade cheesecake which came smothered in raspberries and a pot of pouring cream on the side. After a bit of a struggle they both managed to finish the enormous desserts and then sat back with coffees to let their lunch go down.

'Right, as much as I'd love to sit here all day admiring the view, we'd better call a taxi or we'll be late for the wedding and Andrea will have our guts for garters.'

'I think us not turning up would be one surprise too many after the week they've had' said Sid, calling the waiter over to ask for the bill. 'Now I think everything's done isn't it? Room's paid for and decorated and champagne's been ordered. There wasn't anything else was there?'

'No, I think that's it. I've already let Christos and Anna know that they will be away from the hotel for two nights, although they've most probably let them know now as well, so all we've got to do now is get back and get ready.'

They settled the lunch bill and jumped in the taxi that their waiter had ordered for them, heading back to the Ionian Dream. When they reached the hotel, they went straight to their room for half an hours' lie down before getting ready for the wedding. Waking refreshed and raring to go, they both showered and Elaine, being maid of honour, got ready to take her own outfit and the box containing the brides' dress over to Andrea and Jack's room. Just as she was on her way out, Jack knocked on the door armed with his suit and a bag full of toiletries and the like.

'Ooh, here he is, the bridegroom to be. Not having last minute nerves are you?' laughed Elaine as she let him.

'No, definitely not. I've just been chucked out of my own room to come and get ready with Sid. Not a bad thing though as it's been taken over by loads of women and it already smells like a tart's boudoir. I'd get over there now if I were you as they have already cracked open the bubbly.

Actually it's a shame you didn't get back earlier from town as Anton dropped by the hotel with a couple that he had met on the cruise. He asked me to pass on his love to you both and was sorry he missed you.'

'Oh no, that's typical. The only reason we stayed in town for lunch was so we didn't get in everyone's way. If I'd have known Anton was going to turn up, we would have come back. It's a shame he couldn't come to the wedding really.'

'Yeh it is' agreed Jack. 'Unfortunately his ship was sailing at four o'clock today so he had to get back. But I'm sure we can have a belated celebration next year when we are all out here.'

'Was he enjoying his cruise? Only I know it was the one him and Kenny were supposed to be going on, wasn't it?'

'I think it was. But it definitely sounded like he was having a whale of a time and the couple that he was with, Sally and Mike I think they were called, were a really lovely couple. I'm really pleased that he seems to be moving on with his life after all that tragedy. All we need now is for him to meet someone else and settle down'.

'I think maybe that might be pushing it. Right, I'd better get over to the girls or there will be no bubbly left. Oh and Sid, don't forget the rings, the buttonholes or the groom!'

'No pressure then babes. See you downstairs later. Oh and don't forget the bride'

Elaine left Sid and Jack to it and staggered downstairs to Andrea's room, armed with bags and boxes. Mandy and Sophie were in with Andrea and had already started on the bubbly.

'Blimey, we thought you weren't coming' said Sophie, pouring Elaine a glass of pink champagne. 'Mum was starting to get a bit of a wobble on'

'No I wasn't, cheeky' said Andrea, hitting her daughter on the head with one of the many balloons that were dotted about the bedroom. 'Right now we're all here, and my dress is in one piece I can start to relax. Pass me one of those doughnuts, that

Mandy thoughtfully bought us, before I get dressed, I think I need something to settle my stomach'

'Yeh and to soak up the alcohol' laughed Mandy, as she went to open the door to the hairdresser.

'Afternoon ladies' said the hairdresser as she started to set up her work station, 'now who's first to be transformed?'

For the next couple of hours, Andrea's room was a mass of hairspray, make up and diamantes and soon all four ladies were looking amazing, especially Andrea who had just finished putting on her jewellery when she caught her daughter, sister and best friend staring at her.

'What? Do I look okay?

'Oh Mum you look stunning' said Sophie, her eyes welling up, 'I hope Jack realises how lucky he is'

'I think we're both lucky to have each other sweetheart. Now don't you dare start blubbing or you'll set me off and I'm not about to re-do my make-up. Right, are we all ready? Then let's get this show on the road.'

Jack and Sid were already waiting at the wedding pavilion, along with all the other guests. Jack was dressed in a white linen shirt and trousers, set off with a buttonhole in shades of purple, which co-ordinated beautifully with the attendants' dresses. Sid and the other male guests were also wearing white linen trousers but instead of white shirts, they wore pale lilac ones that Sid had found on-line. After running it past Jack and the other men, he bought the same shirt for each of the men that would be at the ceremony. These shirts were set off by white buttonholes.

The Registrar called Jack and Sid over to the ceremony area as he had just seen the bride and attendants walking through the pavilion to where everyone was now seated, just in front of the pergola.

The pergola, where the actual wedding ceremony would take place, was in the middle of the main pavilion and was a white and blue wooden structure with white washed decking. It was draped with white organza, set off by masses of purple bougainvillea trained around the roof of the pergola. Dotted inside were arrangements of mauve, purple and white freesias, lilies and roses, to match the colour scheme of the bridal party. The guests were all seated in front of the pergola on white chairs that were draped at the back with purple and white chiffon.

Anita was waiting at the entrance of the pavilion to make sure everything was OK with Andrea and to hand out the flowers for the bride and her attendant's. Once everything was in place, Anita signalled to Petros to start up the music. All the guests stood as Andrea and the girls walked through the gardens, to the strains of The Carpenters and "We've only just Begun", to the pergola and the waiting groom and best man.

By the time Andrea had reached Jack, he was a nervous wreck. She took his hand and winked at him, immediately making him feel better, although he did have tears in his eyes when he saw how beautiful she looked.

The service, conducted by a lady Registrar called Maria, was very moving and included readings by Sophie and Elaine, as well as Andrea and Jacks' personalised vows which brought most of the congregation to tears. Once Maria pronounced them man and wife, everyone stood and clapped and the happy couple were led over to the gardens next to main pavilion to have some photos taken of them on their own. The rest of the guests were then called over and the next half an hour or so was spent having group photos with the bride and groom. Once the photographer was certain that he had taken a shot at every angle possible, the guests, were ushered into the pavilion and seated in accordance with the table plan that Anita had situated at the entrance.

Andrea and Jack stayed outside in the gardens for 10 minutes or so to have a few minutes on their own, whilst the waiters poured all their guests a glass of champagne to toast them with when they came in. Petros then tapped the side of a bottle with a knife to get everyone's attention.

'Ladies and gentlemen, please be upstanding for your bride and groom, the new Mr and Mrs Blair.'

Andrea and Jack walked back into the pavilion to a round of applause and as they sat at the head table, a glass of chilled champagne was waiting for each of them and they gratefully had a drink to calm their nerves.

The tables for the wedding breakfast were at the side of the pergola and were also bedecked with the same flowers. They looked beautiful with pristine white tablecloths and white china on gold chargers. Sparkling glass wear and stunning table arrangements completed the striking but classic look that everyone had been striving to achieve.

Jack stood up, glass of champagne in his hand and faced his guests.

'Right, I know this is the part where you're supposed to be bored stupid with a great long speech, but I think we can do without that today. All I really want to say is thank you to Anita and Petros for organising the wedding for us. I think, it goes without saying, that they have done a brilliant job.'

Jack took another quick swig of his bubbly while everyone applauded Anita, Petros and their team.

'OK, I also want to thank the attendants, who look fabulous by the way, and I know Andrea has a little thank you gift for each of you, which I think Anita is just bringing over to you now. Also to my best man, Sid, who I also have a little something for him to say thank you, and to all you lot for coming over sharing this wonderful day with us. I'm sure you don't want me rabbiting on, so without further ado, I'd like to propose a toast to Andrea, my gorgeous bride, who is not only beautiful on the outside but is also a beautiful person on the inside. I love you sweetheart and want you to know that you have made me the happiest person in the world today. Now before I start blubbing, please raise your glasses to Andrea my wonderful wife.'

'Oh and don't forget to toast the groom', said Andrea as she stood up quick with her glass in her hand, 'this man here has made me so happy and I love him to the moon and back. Thank you Jack, for being my husband.'

Everyone raised their glasses and toasted both the bride and groom before Sid got to his feet, glass in hand.

'Right, sorry about this, I know Jack has banned long speeches so I'll keep it short and sweet. All I'm going to say is that I wish both Andrea and Jack all the happiness in the world, they certainly deserve it. I think you'll all agree that the bride and her attendants all look stunning and the whole wedding itself has been seamless, all thanks again to Petros and Anita. So if you can raise your glasses one more time to Jack and Andrea, then I'll let you get on with the task of eating all this delicious food that is waiting to be served.'

Everyone raised their glasses one more time and then sat down as the waiters that were hovering in the wings started bringing through the food.

All three of the girls loved the hand-made necklaces that Andrea had bought for them in Veronica's shop in Zante Town and Sid was over the moon with the Greek flag cufflinks that Jack had bought over from England for him. So that they didn't lose the little boxes, Sid ran upstairs with all the presents and put them in his room for safekeeping. By the time he returned to his table, it was piled high with food.

The wedding breakfast consisted of plates of mixed hors d'oeuvres, including pitta bread and Tzatziki and Hummus, stuffed vine leaves, olives and some mini cheese and spinach pies. The main course was a choice of either Moussaka, Lamb Kleftico or Souvlaki. A large bowl of Greek salad was also placed on each table, as well as jugs of wine, beer and iced water. To finish off the meal, plates of Baklava, Kataifi and slices of water melon were handed round.

A local bouzouki player, dressed in traditional costume, provided the music for the wedding feast and half way through the meal a couple of the waitresses put on an impromptu show by performing a traditional dance.

Coffees were then served, accompanied by Kourabiedes, the traditional Greek wedding cookies. By then everyone was feeling extremely full and a few people went for a little walk in the gardens to walk their dinner off, while the tables were cleared and the DJ set up ready for the evening guests.

'Well I think that went well' said Jack as he and Andrea walked back to their room to freshen up before the evening do.

'I think it went very well' agreed Andrea, linking her arm through Jack's, 'the best day of my life in fact. Anita and Petros really did do us proud, didn't they?

171

The pavilion looked amazing and the food was gorgeous. I can't think of anything that went wrong.'

'No, neither can I and it certainly looks like everyone is enjoying themselves. There was hardly any food left over and the wine bill is growing ever bigger.'

'It's only one day; I really don't think we can begrudge them all a good drink, do you?'

'Oh no, it's good to see all our family and friends having a great time. I think this evening is going to be pretty good as well. It's the same DJ that was on the other night and he managed to get everyone up. Although I think Eddie may have been told to tone it down a bit after his antics at the barbecue.'

'That's a shame' laughed Andrea; I would have loved to have seen him do a repeat performance.

'Well you never know, stranger things have happened. Right, Mrs Blair, if you've finished titivating yourself, we have a wedding reception to go to.'

'Yep, I'm nearly ready. What time have you booked the taxi to take us into town to the Panorama?'

'I booked it for eleven o'clock' said Jack, giving himself a quick blast of body spray, 'I think by then we will be ready to relax a bit on our own. I'll leave our bag by the door and I can pop back and get it just before we go.'

'Right, let's go and see our guests. I haven't had a chance to have a natter to hardly anyone yet.'

Andrea and Jack made their way back to the wedding pavilion where they found that the tables had been cleared and the DJ was just starting up.

'Oh there you are' said Elaine, looking panicked. 'I've been looking everywhere for you. The DJ wants you for the first dance before he can get going. What was the song you wanted again?'

'Tonight I celebrate my love by Peabo Bryson and Roberta Flack' said Andrea, 'I'm sure I already let Petros know that.'

'You most probably did' said Elaine, 'but you know what these Greeks are like, they've most probably never heard of it. You should have told Anita, she'd know it. Anyway it doesn't matter now, I'll just go and let him know and you two can then start the dancing off.'

As the music started up, Andrea and Jack walked out to the compact dance floor for their first dance. Halfway through the song a few more couples had joined them and, after one or two more slow numbers, the DJ put on some Motown classics to get everyone in the party mood.

By eight thirty, the place was rocking. A few more of the guests that Andrea and Jack knew at the hotel had arrived as well as some of the daytime restaurant and bar staff and of course Christos and Anna. Although there were only around thirty five people in attendance, it seemed as though there were a lot more as most people were up dancing.

Sophie had been on the dance floor with Jamie, Stephen and Adam for some time when she decided to go back to her room and change into something cooler as she was getting extremely hot in the long silk dress she was wearing and the high heels she had on were crippling her. She stopped off to chat to her Mum and Jack, who were sitting with Christos, Anna, Anita and Petros.

'Mum, I'm just nipping back upstairs to cool off and change, do you need anything?'

'No, I'm fine Soph thanks. We'll be heading off to Zante Town in about half an hour so don't be too long.'

'Don't worry, I only want to freshen up and put something else on, I won't be ten minutes.'

Sophie went back to her room, had a good old spray of deodorant and perfume and quickly changed into a short cotton dress and flat sandals. As she stood outside her room locking the door, she heard a noise behind her. When she turned round she saw Johnson leaning up against the wall looking her up and down.

'Oh Johnson, it's you. Where did you spring from?' asked Sophie, looking bemused.

'Sorry my dear, did I startle you? I didn't mean to. I was just going up to my room to get my camera and must have come out on the wrong floor. These corridors all look the same. Anyway, now I'm here, why don't you invite me in for a little drink and we can get to know each other better.'

'No, I don't think so' said Sophie, trying to edge herself away from the obviously drunk Johnson.

'Why not, what's wrong with me?'

'Nothing's wrong with you, I just don't want to invite you into my room for a drink. Now can you move so I can go back downstairs with the others?'

'Oh, it's okay to have a drink with that little faggot friend of yours but I'm not good enough, is that it?'

'If you're referring to your cousin Jamie, then yes I am going to have a drink with him and that's really not a nice way to talk about your own flesh and blood is it?'

'You've got to be kidding; he's no relation of mine. Bloody shirt lifter, it's not normal. Now come on love, stop being a little tease and get that door open.'

'How dare you. Who the hell do you think you are? He's more of a man than you'll ever be. Now get out of my way before I call security.'

As Sophie went to walk past Johnson he grabbed her arm and pulled her back towards him. As he did so, Adam happened to walk round the corner and saw Sophie struggling to get away from him.

'Oi mate, what the hell do you think you're doing? Get your hands off her before I ram my fist down your throat.'

Adam grabbed hold of Johnson and shoved him out of the way.

'Are you alright Soph?'

'Yeh, I'm fine Adam, thanks' said Sophie, looking a little bit shaken.

'Come on, let's go back down to the reception and get a drink before I knock this idiot out.'

'I didn't mean any harm Sophie' cried Johnson as they walked away. 'I was only trying to be friendly. Please don't tell anyone about this.'

'Yeh whatever, bully boy. Go and play with the traffic while you still can, and next time pick on someone your own size'

Sophie looked completely relieved to be away from Johnson, 'I don't know what would have happened if you hadn't come along, he really was getting a big aggressive. Thanks ever so much for stepping in.'

'My pleasure. Always been a bit of a sucker for a Sheila in distress. Now let's go and get this drink.'

As they walked back into the pavilion, Lizzie noticed how close Adam was starting to get to Sophie. She would definitely have to keep an eye on those two.

At around eleven o'clock the DJ announced that it was time for the bride and groom to get their taxi to Zante Town. Andrea and Jack went round the room saying their goodbyes to everyone and thanking them all for coming to their wedding.

'Blimey girl, you're only going down the road for a couple of nights' laughed Sid as Andrea started to cry when she hugged him and Elaine.

'I know, but we wouldn't be going there at all if it wasn't for you two. I can't believe how lucky we are to have two friends as good as you. I do love you both.'

'Right, come on Mrs B' said Jack, taking Andrea's arm, 'I think someone may have had a touch too much champagne. It's a good job we are only going down the road. But she is right; we really do appreciate everything you've done for us.'

'Go on, off with you both before we start welling up' said Elaine, giving Jack a hug. 'Have a fabulous time and we'll see you back here Monday sometime. I'm sure you won't miss anything here.'

'Ha, famous last words' laughed Jack. 'I'm sure we'll have a marvellous time, we'll text you to let you know how it's going.'

Andrea and Jack left to collect their bag from the room and get the taxi to Zante Town, leaving Elaine, Sid and the rest of the guests still partying.

The reception went on to about midnight, when the DJ finally called it a night due to noise restrictions. Some of the guests were still milling about in the pavilion until around one in the morning, whilst others took themselves back up to the main hotel bar to carry on drinking. It wasn't until gone four o'clock that the last guest had finally retired to bed.

Saturday 13th September

There were a lot of sore heads and delicate stomachs that morning at breakfast and Elaine and Sid's were no exception. As they sat under the shade with some toast and coffee contemplating the day ahead, Sophie and Mandy appeared and joined them.

'Morning ladies, you both look surprisingly restored from last night, unlike us two' said Sid from behind his dark glasses.

'Believe it or not I was pretty sober' said Sophie, 'unlike Auntie Mandy here, who was completely plastered but, for some unknown reason, doesn't seem to have any side effects. How is that possible exactly?'

'Years of experience, Soph' laughed Mandy, 'so, what are you two up to today? I bet you're lost without the happy couple, aren't you?'

'You're right, it does seem weird without them' agreed Elaine, gingerly nibbling on a slice of toast and honey, 'although we had a text from them just before we came out of the room, saying that they had got there okay and to thank us for doing up the room, which was nice. But, in answer to your question, I think we'll just stay round the pool today. I don't think I've got the energy to walk down to the beach and, if my head doesn't feel much better, I may even have a sleep back in the room later on. What are you two doing then?'

'I think we might have a walk down the beach this morning and check out some of the bars down the other end' said Sophie, tucking into a plate of eggs and bacon. 'We were going to ask Jamie and Stephen if they wanted to come with us but poor old Jamie really is suffering after last night and they've gone back to bed. I think Adam may come with us though.'

'He's a nice lad, that Adam isn't he?' said Sid, pouring himself some more coffee.

'Yeh, he's a really lovely bloke' agreed Sophie.

'Ooh, she loves him' laughed Mandy.

'Shut up you, it's not like that, we're just friends'

'I think the lady doth protest too much' said Sid, laughing as Sophie went bright red. 'Right, go on you two, sod off to the beach and give me and Elaine a bit of peace and quiet. I'm sure we'll see you later.'

'Oh, actually I did mean to ask you Elaine' said Sophie, finishing the last of her bacon. 'we're going to Zorba's tonight for dinner, do you and Sid fancy joining us? Jamie and Stephen will be coming, as long as their hangovers have gone and so will Adam and his mum and dad.'

'That'd be nice, we haven't been there yet this year so yes, as long as my head has recovered, we'll definitely join you. I do love it in there'.

Sophie and Mandy finished off their coffees and left Elaine and Sid sitting at the table nursing their headaches.

'I don't know about you babe' said Elaine rubbing her temples, 'but I think I may go back to the room now for a nap. Hopefully, after a couple of hours sleep we may feel better.'

'Yeh, I think you're right' agreed Sid, putting down a half-eaten brioche. 'A couple of paracetamols, washed down with a pint of water and some sleep should sort us out. Perhaps then we might feel like eating something as well, because I certainly can't at the moment.'

Elaine and Sid made their way back to their room, drew the curtains, put on the air-con and flopped back into bed. They both slept until lunchtime when they woke up feeling one hundred percent better and totally ravenous. Jumping quickly in the shower to freshen up, they put on some clean clothes and went down to the pool bar to order some much needed food.

There didn't seem to be anyone else from their party around the pool, which suited Elaine and Sid as they hadn't had a lot of time on their own recently. Desperately in need of some stodge, they ordered double cheese and bacon burger, a meat feast pizza and a large plate of chips. Their order came pretty quickly and they tucked in greedily.

'Oh, this is so good', said Elaine with her mouth full of pizza, 'I feel so much better already, I think we'll definitely go to Zorba's tonight with the other, just cut back on the booze a bit.'

'You say that now' laughed Sid, just about to take an enormous mouthful of his cheeseburger, 'but wait until the girls start on the cocktails. You know you won't be able to refuse.'

'Yes, I know. I've got no willpower; tell me something I don't know. Can I try a bit of your burger?'

'No, eat your own' said Sid as he pulled the half eaten burger towards him, 'you always do that. Oh go on then, just a little bit. I should know by now you always get your own way.'

They both finished their food and made their way over to the pool where they managed to bag a couple of sun loungers in the shade. Setting their towels out and stripping down to their swimwear, they laid round the pool snoozing and reading until they saw Jamie and Stephen making their way over to them.

'Blimey, don't tell me you two have just got up' said Sid, sitting up and putting on his sunglasses.

'No, we got up a couple of hours ago' said Jamie, plonking himself on Elaine's sun bed, 'Stephen had to pop in the supermarket for some more mozzie repellent so we stopped off at the bakery next door for something to eat.'

'They do some nice stuff in there, don't they?' said Elaine

'Tell me about it' said Stephen, pulling up another sun bed to sit on 'we had a couple of warm cheese pies, which were delicious, and then we shared a massive piece of chocolate gateaux. I'm absolutely stuffed now. So what have you two been doing then, just laying round here all day?'

'No, we actually went back to bed after breakfast as well. Got up around lunchtime and had something to eat at the pool bar and have been over here ever since. I think most of us were suffering a bit this morning but it was worth it though, wasn't it?'

'Oh definitely' agreed Jamie, 'the wedding was brilliant and Dad and Andrea looked amazing. I'm so pleased for them both; they deserve a happy ever after. I must admit, after the shock of seeing my mother after all these years the other night, I did think it might have jinxed the day but luckily it went without a hitch.'

'That really was a turn up for the books, wasn't it Jamie' said Sid, 'who would have thought that your mum would have been out here all this time, right under our noses. It really is a small world sometimes.'

'Do you remember anything about your mum before she left home?' asked Elaine.

'No, not really, I was only a little boy. It was Luke that it affected the most, as he was older. I'm glad he wasn't here to have seen her as I don't think he would have coped very well.'

'I was surprised how well you coped really, considering the shock it must have been.'

'Yeh, so was I' laughed Jamie. 'I had sometimes wondered what I would do if I came face to face with her again but, I must admit, I hadn't reckoned on that scenario! I was shocked and maybe a little bit curious at first, but then I remembered what she put my dad and Luke through and any feelings I may have had for her completely went out of the window. I wasn't joking when I said that Andrea had been more of a mother to me than that woman ever was, because she has. I think the world of Andrea and I think Luke does too, and I'm sure he would rather her be a grandmother to his new baby than some woman who just happened to give birth to him. Right, I'm glad I got that off my chest. Who wants a swim?'

All talk of Veronica/Diane finished and the four of them got in the pool, where they somehow managed to get roped into a game of water ping pong with another couple that they knew from the hotel. After an hour or so of jumping around in the pool and getting decidedly wrinkly, they got out and lay in the sun for a while to dry off. Sid went and got some glasses of freshly squeezed orange juice for them and talk turned to that evening.

'So have Sophie and Mandy spoken to you about going to Zorba's tonight?' said Jamie, after taking a refreshing swig of his drink.

'Yeh, they mentioned it this morning at breakfast' said Elaine, 'although I think it was dependent on the state of everyone's hangover, but as we all seem to be back in the land of the living, I assume we will be going there. You haven't been there yet, have you?'

'No, Sophie was telling me about it last night. She said her mum's always going on about it, so we thought we'd better try it out.'

'You'll love it' said Sid, 'they've got a great menu plus there's always entertainment of some sort. The waiters do some Greek dancing with a difference and they get all the kids up to smash the plates. They are a great bunch of lads that work there. Right, I don't know about you lot but I've had enough sun now, I think I'll head on up to the room for a shower. Shall we meet you two in the bar about half seven tonight?'

'Sounds like a plan, Sid' said Stephen, getting a book out of his bag, 'I think we'll have another half an hour or so and then go up and get ready, so we'll see you both later.'

Elaine and Sid went back up to their room and after a cup of tea and a couple of biscuits on the balcony while they were catching up with Facebook and uploading some more of the photos that they took at the wedding, they both had showers, put on their glad rags and went downstairs to the bar to meet with the others.

They were the first to get in the bar and Sid ordered Elaine and himself a couple of gin and tonics and sat up the bar to chat to Petros. Within minutes they were joined by Sophie, Mandy and Adam, closely followed by Lizzie and Raymond. Everyone got a drink and moved over to a large table next to the bar while they waited for Jamie and Stephen. They didn't have to wait long before the boys turned up and, after everyone had finished their drinks, they made their way down the road to Zorba's Restaurant.

Zorba's, was one of the bigger restaurants in the resort and had a large outside dining area, flanked by gardens, which lead up to the main restaurant. It held over a hundred people at any given time and employed around a dozen waiting staff, most of who were running around with various dishes and tray of drinks in the already busy restaurant.

'Blimey, this looks busy, we'll be lucky if we get a table tonight' said Mandy, already checking out the waiters.

'Oh ye of little faith' said Sid, waving to one of the waiters, who was already on his way over to them.

'Hey Sid, Elaine, how are you both? Your table is all ready for you, just over here.'

'Thanks Michaelos. It's good to be back. How's everything been?'

'Really good, thanks. As you can see we are really busy and have been all season, so everyone's happy. Where's Jack and Andrea, not with you this year?'

'Of course they are. They got married yesterday at the hotel and we treated them to a couple of nights in Zante Town as a mini honeymoon. We'll be back with them before we go and I'm sure they'll want to see you. Right, this is Jack's son, Jamie and his partner Stephen'

Sid continued to introduce everyone to the owner of Zorba's and then ordered a round of drinks while they perused the menus.

'Did you book a table for tonight Sid?' asked Mandy, pouring her and Sophie a glass of red.

'Of course I did. I messaged Michaelos this morning after you mentioned it at breakfast. I knew they got busy really quickly so I thought if I didn't book something we would never have got in. If we hadn't felt up to it, I could have easily messaged him again to cancel.'

'It's a good job we've got someone sensible here then' laughed Sophie.

'I wouldn't go that far' said Elaine, ducking as Sid flicked a piece of bread at her. 'Oh here comes Michaelos with his pad, does everyone know what they are having?'

They all gave Michaelos their orders and before long plates of delicious looking food were coming their way from the kitchen. Sid, Raymond, Adam and Mandy had all ordered the Kleftico, which came complete with its own light show. One of the waiters brought a tray of flaming foil packages from the kitchen and stood at the table while the obligatory photos were taken. The packages, still flaming, were then then put on plates on the table and opened to reveal a parcel of lamb, potatoes, herbs and feta cheese.

'Wow, these look amazing' said Adam, breathing in the tempting aromas that were coming out of the parcels, 'what have the rest of you got?'

'Well, I've got Moussaka' said Sophie.

'Me and Stephen have got mixed souvlaki with chips and a Greek salad' said Elaine, and I think your mum's got some sort of beef in a pot, by the looks of things'

'Beef Stamnas, I think it's called' said Lizzie tucking in, 'and very nice it is too.'

'And last but not least, Jamie's got Calamari' said Elaine 'which is very good because I've just nicked a bit.'

Everyone thoroughly enjoyed their meals and the waiters collected completely empty plates. They all, apart from Mandy, ordered some desserts and coffee and liqueurs for afterwards. As they were waiting for their desserts to arrive, some of the waiters came out front and put on a little show of Greek dancing that included dancing around circles of fire that one of the waiters was creating by shooting lines of paraffin across the floor. They then got some of the customers up with them to dance as well. Raymond, Mandy, Sid and Jamie all got up and had go at doing the Sirtaki, a popular Greek dance done at most social functions, while Elaine stood and videoed it all on her phone, ready to put on-line when she got back to the hotel. They came back to the table, totally exhausted, just as desserts were being served.

'Oh my God, how much fun was that' said Mandy, fanning herself with a drinks mat, 'and how fit was that waiter? I certainly wouldn't kick him out of bed!'

'Oh leave it out Auntie Mandy' said Sophie looking shocked, 'you're old enough to be his mum and he's really creepy.'

'You're right Soph, he is a bit smarmy,' agreed Elaine, 'I think you could do a bit better than that Mandy.'

Michaelos came over to the table, pulled a chair up and sat down next to Sid.

'Okay, how was the food everyone?'

They all agreed that the food was amazing and sent their compliments to the chef, saying that they had all had a fabulous evening.

'Good, that's what we like to hear. Now, what would everyone like as a drink on the house?'

Michaelos went round the table taking the drinks order, while they all watched as a couple of the waiters brought half a dozen young children up to the front of the restaurant so they could smash some plates on the floor.

'That looks fun' said Adam, 'do you think they'd let me have a go?'

'No Adam' laughed Lizzie, 'I think you'll find it's for small children only.'

'Oh mum that's so unfair. My evening is ruined now'

Adam stamped his feet and put on his best pout, causing everyone to burst out laughing.

Once Michaelos had handed out everyone's drinks, Raymond tapped his glass to get everyone's attention.

'Right, I'm sure you'll all agree that tonight has been a really lovely evening, in fact the whole holiday so far has been amazing, and I'd just like to propose a toast to fabulous family, friends and good times.'

Everyone raised their glasses in a toast just as Elaine's phone beeped.

She laughed as she read the text that had just come through.

'How spooky is that' she said 'I've just had a text from Andrea saying they are having a fabulous meal in the hotel restaurant and have just raised their glasses, filled with the champagne that Mandy arranged for them, to their wonderful friends and family. She also said that they would be back here around tea time tomorrow'

'Blimey, that is weird' said Raymond, 'but at least we know they are having a great time. Now who's up for another drink?'

'You know what, I think we'll stop while the going's good' said Sid, finishing off his brandy from Michaelos.

'Yeh, I make you right' agreed Elaine. 'I feel just comfortable now and I certainly don't want another hangover like I had this morning, so I think we'll call it a night if you don't mind.'

The others ordered some more drinks but Elaine and Sid gave Raymond their share of the bill and made their way back to the hotel. Even going without their obligatory cuppa on the balcony, they both got changed, fell into bed and were both in the land of nod before the others had even left the restaurant.

Sunday 14th September

The next morning Elaine and Sid woke up quite early and, after a full night's sleep, they felt great.

'I'm so glad we came back to the room when we did' said Elaine getting dressed. 'I feel completely refreshed this morning but I think it would have been a different matter if we'd have stayed. I wonder what time the others got back last night.'

'I dread to think. No doubt there'll be some more hangovers this morning. Right, what do you fancy doing this morning, beach or pool?'

'The beach I think, we haven't been down there for a while and I really need to start concentrating on my tan. Andrea and Jack aren't coming back until later on this afternoon now, so we can meet up with them when we get back'

'Okay, do you fancy missing out breakfast in case we get caught up round the pool? We can grab a bacon sarnie and a coffee at Spiros and it would be lovely to be the first on the beach when it's lovely and quiet.'

'That sounds perfect babe' said Elaine, 'I'll just put our beach stuff in the bag and we can get off.'

There was no sign of anyone as they walked through reception and out onto the road. In fact they didn't pass another soul until they got almost level with Spiro's van.

'Oh my God, you are early today' said Spiro, who was still setting out his van. 'I take it you're on your own.'

'I'm afraid so Spiro, Andrea and Jack are still staying at the hotel in Zante Town and we've left everyone else in bed I think. We fancied getting down here early and having a full day on the beach. We haven't even had any breakfast so I don't suppose you can do us a couple of bacon rolls and cappuccino's?'

'Certainly Sid, give me ten minutes to get the grill on and you can have them. Why don't you go down and get your sun bed and by the time you get back we'll be cooking.'

So, Elaine and Sid went down to the beach and had the pick of any sun bed they wanted. They claimed two beds that were set a bit away from the others so as to get a bit of peace and quiet. After putting their towels down and getting out their sun creams and books, they walked back up to Spiros where, sure enough the smell of bacon was drifting out of the van, making them both salivate.

'That smells so good Spiros' said Sid, taking the lid off his coffee to add some sugar.

'I aim to please' grinned Spiros, piling crispy bacon into two enormous baguettes. 'Now do you want sauce on these or just plain?'

'I'll have mine plain please Spiros but you'd better ruin Sid's by putting some tomato ketchup on it.'

'Ruin it' said Sid, 'you don't know what you're talking about woman. It enhances the taste.'

'Yeh, whatever. I prefer the taste of bacon myself' said Elaine, pulling a face at Spiros squirting the ketchup all over Sid's breakfast.

They took their rolls and coffees, paid Spiros and went back down to the beach where they sat on their sunbeds to eat breakfast.

'This is the life, eh Laney' said Sid, having taken a large bite of his roll.

'It certainly is babes. I think I could get used to this. It's a shame we have to go home at the end of the week, I could stay here forever.'

'You say that now, but I bet you wouldn't be so keen in the winter when it's wet and windy and everything's shut up. And don't forget there's no Lakeside for you to go shopping or theatres and concert venues. You'd go stir crazy within a month.'

'I never really thought about that. Perhaps we'll stick with coming here for holidays then. Oh look there's Mick' said Elaine waving over a burly looking bloke who was power walking along the beach with his headphones on.

'Hiya Mick, long time, no see, how are you? When did you get here?'

'Hey, hello you. I thought I was the only one that got up with the lark. We got here last night and by the colour of you two, you've been here a while.'

'Yeh, we've been here over a week now' said Elaine. 'Well it's great seeing you again. No doubt we'll see you and Annie again at the hotel. I'll let you get back to your walking. Take care.'

'Oh I will, don't worry. I don't want a repeat performance of last year and have to ask people to pee on me!'

Elaine laughed as Mick went walking back up the beach and Sid looked at Elaine in confusion.

'Sorry, but what the hell was that all about and who is that bloke?'

'That's Mick. He comes out here with his wife, Annie. They are staying at our hotel, you must have seen him'

'I might have, but how do you know him and what's with the peeing over him thing?'

'He's been coming to the hotel for a few years now but I've never really spoken to him, until last year. You must remember, it was here on the beach and he got stung by a jellyfish. I told him that I had something that he could put on it and that it didn't involve peeing on him. I remember he was in a lot of pain but did laugh at that. Every time I saw him in the hotel after that he mentioned it.'

'Oh yeh, I remember now. Didn't you lend him the cream I brought for some bites I had? His wife took the name of it and went and got some from the chemist.'

'That's them. It's a bit of a standing joke now. I wonder if it is true that urine takes the sting out of jellyfish stings. I must admit I've never seen anyone do it, have you?'

'No, can't say that I have' said Sid, getting up to go in the sea. 'Anyway, all this talk has made me want to go now. Last one in buys the lunch.'

After a few hours on the beach they finally decided to go back to the hotel around 3 o'clock. Walking back through the pool area to the hotel, they saw Sophie, Mandy and the three lads looking very conspiratory. Mandy started frantically waving when she saw Elaine and Sid heading their way.

'Where have you two been all day?' she said excitedly, 'You've missed all the fun here.'

'We've been on the beach all day' said Elaine, 'so come on, what's been happening? What have we missed?'

'You're not going to believe it,' said Sophie but there was a big commotion earlier when this Greek bloke came marching into the hotel accusing one of the guests of assaulting his daughter.'

'Blimey, it all happens here doesn't it' said Sid, 'did they find the bloke who done it.'

'Well, that's where the fun begins' said Jamie, 'it only turned out to be my lovely, homophobic cousin, Johnson. Seems like he had started chatting up this girl who worked in a bar and then touched her up. When she told him to leave her alone and get out of the bar, he slapped her and called her a whore, or words to that effect. What he didn't realise was, her brother was working behind the bar and saw everything. He got his dad and they both came here looking for him.'

'No way,' said Elaine, 'he is a bit of a prat but do you think he would have done something like that?'

'Oh yes, he definitely would.' said Adam.

Everyone looked at Adam in confusion at how he would think that.

'Look, I know Sophie didn't want to tell anyone but I caught him trying it on with her at Andrea and Jack's wedding.'

'You're kidding. Is that true Sophie?' said Elaine looking really concerned, 'why didn't you say anything. Your mum and Jack would have gone mad if they'd have known.'

'That's exactly why I didn't say anything, especially at their wedding. I will tell them when they get back later though.'

'So what happened then?'

'You remember how hot it was that night in those dresses of ours? Well, I went back to the room and got changed into something cooler to dance in and when I came back out of the room, Johnson was standing there saying something about he had come out on the wrong floor. He asked if he could come in for a drink and I told him absolutely not. Then he started to get nasty, saying that I'd drink with my little faggot friend, meaning Jamie, but not him. I told him to get lost and he went to grab me. That's when Adam happened to come along, thank God, otherwise I dread to think what he would have done. Adam pulled him out of the way and told him in no uncertain terms that if he came near me again he would shove his fist down his throat. To be fair, I thought it was just the drink that had made him like it and didn't really think much more of it, but when this happened this afternoon it became obvious that this is something he does on a regular basis.'

'Your mum and Jack will be back soon and you can tell them what happened to you and about his little escapade with the girl in the bar. I'm sure Jack will be wanting to have a little word with his brother and his pervert of a nephew. I must admit, he's always given me the creeps and I know you didn't like him, did you Sid?'

'No, I thought he was a jumped up little shit. It's about time someone brought him down a peg or two.'

205

'Well actually they did' said Sophie grinning. 'When the girl's dad asked about him, obviously Christos couldn't give him Johnson's room number but, as luck would have it, he just happened to walk through the reception area as they were talking and the girl's dad recognised him straight away. They ran outside after him and the dad got him up against the wall by his throat and threatened him. When he let him go, Johnson must have said something sarcastic, because one of the Greek blokes turned back and lamped him one. He's got a fabulous black eye now.'

'Bloody brilliant' said Elaine laughing, 'I wonder how he's going to explain that to mummy dearest.'

'After my dad's finished with him, she'll be the last of his worries' said Jamie 'That'll teach him for calling me a dirty little faggot.'

'You're absolutely right Jamie and it couldn't happen to a nicer person' said Elaine, getting her key out of her bag. 'Right, we're going on up to get showered and changed. What's everyone up to tonight?'

'We were only talking about that before you two turned up' said Sophie, 'There's an English singer playing in one of the bars down the strip. He's supposed to be really good so we thought we'd have something to eat in the restaurant next door and then have a couple of drinks and listen to some live music. Are you two up for it?'

'Sounds like a plan' said Sid, 'it'll make a change to get some decent entertainment and your mum and Jack will like that as well. Are you sure us oldies won't cramp your style?'

'No, don't be stupid, of course you won't. We wouldn't ask you if we didn't want your company. Now, mum and Jack will be back any minute so we'll wait around for them and let them know what's happened with Johnson and then we can all meet back down here in the bar in a couple of hours, if that's okay?'

'Yeh, that's fine as long as Jack hasn't been arrested for killing Johnson in the meantime!'

'Don't worry Sid; I'll keep an eye on my dad. I'm sure he'll just want to let Edison sort his own son out but I'll stay with him just in case.'

'Good lad. Right we'll see you lot later.'

Elaine and Sid went up to their room to chill out for an hour or so and then get ready for that evening. They had only been gone ten minutes or so when Andrea and Jack arrived back at the hotel. As soon as they saw Sophie, Jamie and the others huddled together chatting, they knew something had happened.

'Hello you lot,' said Jack, dumping his case on the floor 'we didn't expect a welcoming committee but it's nice of you to come and wait for us to get back. In fact you can carry this up to our room, Jamie. As you can see, us newlyweds are finding it a bit difficult to walk at the moment!'

'Eugh, too much information' said Sophie with a look of horror on her face.'

'Take no notice of him Sophie' said Andrea laughing, 'the only reason we are finding it difficult to walk is because we went on one of those jeep safaris yesterday and our backs are bloody killing us now. You should have seen us last night; we were walking about like a couple of eighty year olds. I don't think either of us will be seeing much action anywhere else for a while yet.'

'Okay mum, I get the idea! Anyway, apart from almost killing yourselves, did you have a good time?'

'Oh yes, it was a lovely couple of days. That hotel is gorgeous. Elaine and Sid had only booked us the honeymoon suite. It was amazing with a four poster bed and a Jacuzzi, which definitely came in handy when we got back from that blasted jeep safari. The restaurant there is really good as well. We only had one meal there, apart from breakfast, and we went into town the rest of the time. I still can't get over how good it was of them to treat us. Talking of which, where are Elaine and Sid?'

'You've just missed them' said Jamie, 'they've only just gone up to their room. We said we'd wait down here for you to get back and fill you in on everything that's happened.'

'Well that should take all of thirty seconds then' laughed Jack.

'Ah, that's where you're wrong dad, it's all been happening here. Let's sit down and get some drinks and we can tell you all the news.'

Adam went to the bar and got a round of drinks in while the others found a quiet table on the terrace to sit at. Once the drinks had been handed out, Jamie, Sophie and the others relayed what had happened with Johnson. Jack didn't look too surprised and actually laughed when Stephen told them about Johnson getting a black eye from one of the Greeks that had come looking from him. It was only when Sophie and Adam relayed what had happened to her on the wedding night that the mood changed.

'He did what?' fumed Jack, 'why didn't you tell us sooner?'

'Because it was your wedding night and I didn't want to put a damper on it. Anyway, Adam had it covered and he didn't actually do anything to me.'

'Yes, but he might have done if Adam hadn't come along when he did' said Andrea, 'I've never liked the little shit but I honestly didn't think he was capable of doing something like this. I've a good mind to go and find him myself and give him another black eye to match the one he's already got.'

'I honestly don't think he's worth wasting your energy on' said Sophie, 'I think the best thing to do is have it out with him in front of Caroline and Edison. She thinks the sun shines out of his backside, and it's about time she knew what he was really like.'

'You're right Sophie, let's wait until they are all together and then bring it up. I'd love to bring them all down a peg or two. I know he's my brother but he can't keep lying to Caroline and getting that son of his out of trouble, it's about time they all knew what he's like. Now, what are we all doing tonight?'

After finishing their drinks, they all went to their respective rooms to get ready for that evening.

They met back in the bar at around seven thirty and had just the one drink each. There was no sign of Johnson or his parents and Lizzie and Raymond had decided to eat at the hotel as they were still tired from a day trip they had been on.

The restaurant they had decided to eat in was called The Garden Restaurant and it was a five minute walk from the hotel. They managed to get a table for nine quite easily and decided to order a selection of different dishes and share. On the table, amongst other things, where was a huge Greek

211

salad, pitta and a selection of dips, calamari, meatballs, ribs, lamb chops and chips. To wash it all down, carafes of village wine were dotted around the table. They all ate hungrily and, in between mouthfuls, chattered about the wedding and what Andrea and Jack had got up to while they were in Zante Town.

After they had finished eating, they paid the bill and decamped next door at the Nirvana Bar, which was quite a large bar that regularly hosted live entertainment. It generally got busier after about ten when the entertainment started, which meant it didn't really interfere with people dining next door as most people had finished their meals by then. Elaine had already told them that the bar was normally pretty busy later on so they got in there by nine o'clock to grab some decent seats. They managed to get a couple of tables to push together almost in front of the stage where the entertainment would be.

'So who's this bloke that's singing here tonight then?' asked Sid.

'I think his name is Justin Hayes' said Sophie, 'he's supposed to be pretty good and does a wide range of genres, so we'll see. If he's no good we can always go somewhere else.'

'Justin Hayes' said Sid, 'I've got a feeling I know him, if it's the same bloke, although I can't think there's too many Justin Hayes around.'

'I think you're right' agreed Elaine, 'isn't he the bloke who used to play at The Plough down the road from us?'

'Yeh, that's the one babe. If it is him, then he's really good and a really nice bloke. Comes from Billericay if I remember. Fancy him ending up out here. It really is a small world sometimes.'

They all ordered cocktails from the extensive list that the very knowledgeable barman brought over and then sat and waited for the singer to come on. When he walked through to set his mike up, Sid noticed that it was in fact the Justin Hayes that he knew and he waved him over to where they were sitting.

'Hey Sid, Elaine. Fancy seeing you two here'

Justin came over and shook Sid's hand and gave Elaine a peck on the cheek.

'Alright mate, how's it going? When we were told who was singing tonight we did wonder if it was you and, sure enough, here you are. What made you want to come out here and sing?'

'Hello Sid, have a look around you' said Justin, sweeping his arm around the bar. 'Where would you rather be cold and wet Billericay or here in Zante? I've got some good gigs around the island and work nearly every night. During the day I can lay on the beach, go swimming, meet up with friends. It's a no brainer.'

'I make you right mate' said Sid, 'I know what I'd rather do. Sorry, where's my manners, let me introduce you to everyone.'

Once Sid had the introductions out of the way, Justin was almost ready to go on.

'It's lovely to see you Sid and everyone else but unfortunately I've got to do some work now. I'll pop back over and chat some more when I take a break'

Justin got on stage and introduced himself and then launched into his first song of the evening. Within minutes the first of many people got up and started dancing. Before long he had quite a crowd of dancers in front of him.

'You were right Sid, he is a really good singer' said Mandy, who hadn't taken her eyes off him. 'He's also really hot. Do you know if he's single?'

'No idea Mandy. I think he did have a girlfriend when he played at the Plough but that was quite a while ago so I wouldn't have a clue now.'

'Don't you think he's a bit young for you Mandy' said Andrea

'Cheeky mare, there can't be a lot of difference in our ages.'

'I think you'll find there is' said Sid, 'you're late forties and Justin's only about thirty, maybe thirty two.'

'Yeh, but I don't look that old though, do I?'

Everyone just looked at Mandy in disbelief.

'What? You can all be very hurtful sometimes, and you can stop bloody laughing Andrea, it's not funny.'

'Yeh, it is Mandy, sorry.'

'Right, I'm going to have a dance, who's joining me? Or am I too old to be able to dance as well?'

Sophie, Jamie and Adam all got up to dance with Mandy while the others sat back and listened to the soulful voice of Justin. After a few more cocktails, everyone was in a party mood and at one time even Sid and Jack got up for a boogie. After Justin had finished his performance and the bar switched to piped music, he came and sat down with Sid and the rest of them for a while and then moved to the bar where he was chatting to the barman. Mandy, at this point, was completely drunk and trying to get off with a bemused Justin, to the amusement of everyone else in the bar.

'Oh God, look at my sister' said Andrea rolling her eyes upward, 'she's absolutely legless and she's all over that poor singer. She really is a complete embarrassment.'

'She's not hurting anyone mum' said Sophie, 'let her have some fun, she's on her holidays.'

'I know sweetheart, but unfortunately your Auntie Mandy never knows when to stop and then everyone else has to pick up the pieces. But, hey ho, you're right she is on her holidays so let her get on with it.'

Jamie and Stephen got up and said their goodbyes as they had to be up early the next morning to go on a boat trip.

'Flipping hell, it's gone half past one in the morning' said Elaine, looking at her watch in horror, 'I didn't think it was that late. We'd better get going back to the hotel.'

'Why?' asked Adam. 'Have you got to get up for work in the morning or something?'

'No, but it's very late.'

'You're on your holidays' sang everyone round the table.

'No, you're right. Sod it; let's have another one of those Pina Coladas.'

After another round of drinks they were all ready to walk back to the hotel, even a very drunk Mandy who had just seen how stunning Justin's Greek girlfriend was and had finally admitted defeat.

The hotel bar was closed and in darkness when they got back so they all called it a night and went up to their rooms, trying not to make too much noise in the process.

Monday 15th September

The next morning was an absolute scorcher and although the outlook was for rain and storms nobody seemed to take much notice as there wasn't a cloud in the sky.

Nearly everyone decided to have a day by the pool, apart from Jamie and Stephen who had booked to go on a boat trip. There had been no sightings of Johnson or his mum and dad, although everyone had kept an eye out for them as Jack was desperate to let the cat out of the bag about Johnson's wrongdoings.

Surprisingly, considering how late they were out the night before, no-one really had a hangover. Elaine and Andrea were tired but that wasn't unusual for them. Anything past nine in the evening and they were tired the next morning lately.

After hearty breakfasts all round, everyone got into position round the pool ready for a day of serious sunbathing. Within minutes of putting their stuff down, Lizzie and Raymond decided to go off for a walk and then Sophie and Adam announced that it was too quiet round the pool for them and they were going to try a hotel down the road that was hosting water volley competitions and was a bit more lively.

'So much for a family day round the pool then' laughed Andrea as they all disappeared, leaving just the five of them still laying on their sun beds.

'So have you actually been down to the beach yet Mandy?' asked Elaine as she slathered factor thirty over herself.

'No, I'm not a great lover of the sea. I feel a lot safer in the pool, especially after Sid told me about those fish. There's no way I'd go in the sea with them about.'

'What those little tiny fishes that you get at the shore line. I'm not sure what they're called but they're only tiny and won't hurt you.'

'No, not those. It's the big one's that attack your privates, so Sid said.'

'You don't mean the willy fish do you?' said Elaine, looking over at Andrea and the pair of them collapsing in a heap with laughter.

'What's so funny about that? Sid said they were really dangerous, didn't you?' said Mandy to Sid who had now joined in with the girls' laughter.

'Oh Mandy, I can't believe you fell for that old chestnut' said Andrea, wiping the tears of laughter from her face. 'The willy fish isn't real; it's just something Sid made up. We were all in the sea one day messing about and Sid took off his swimming shorts and started chasing me and Elaine, shouting "the willy fish is gonna get you" and it sort of stuck. I can't believe you haven't been in the sea because you believed it was a proper fish.'

'Well how was I to know' said Mandy, looking a bit miffed, as everyone started laughing again. 'That's it; all have a good giggle at my expense. It's about time you lot grew up and acted your age.'

'Ooh, someone's got the hump' laughed Sid, 'not my fault if you're gullible is it and anyway why would you be worried about the willy fish, it's not like you've got a willy! Oh go on, crack your dial and see the funny side of it.'

'Whatever. I'm going over to sit with Maggie and Susan. At least they won't make a laughing stock out of me.'

Mandy picked up her things and moved to the other side of the pool to sit with her two friends, scowling at Sid as she went.

'Blimey, I'm right in her bad books. She's giving me daggers.'

'Oh well, I'm sure you're not going to lose any sleep over it Sid. My sister really needs to get a sense of humour sometimes. She can give it but she can't take it. But that was funny though, I'd actually forgotten all about the willy fish.'

Elaine, who seemed to be sweating profusely, got up from her sun bed and moved it under the umbrella. 'Oh, I don't know about you Andrea, but I'm sweating buckets up here. There's no breeze at all.'

'I was just thinking the same thing. It's so humid. Do you fancy going for a walk down to the beach, at least there's a bit of a breeze down there? What do you reckon lads, stay here or go down to the beach?'

'I think we'd definitely be better off down the beach. I'm baking here' said Sid, getting his stuff together. 'Do you think Mandy will want to come with us?'

'No, I think she may give that a miss' laughed Andrea 'but I will just nip over and tell where we're going though'.

Once Andrea had let Mandy know where they were going and they had got their stuff together, they trotted off to the beach.

They could hear the sea before they reached Spiros' van, which was quite worrying as it was normally so calm. What was also worrying was the mass of black clouds that had suddenly appeared over the hills of Laganas and which seemed to be headed their way.

'Blimey, I don't like the look of that sky' said Jack, looking quite worried, 'and can you hear the sea, it sounds a bit rough to me.'

'Oh don't be a wuss' said Elaine, 'it's only a few clouds, they'll soon get burned off by the sun and the sea's most probably rough because of a storm out at sea or something. Don't worry it will be fine.'

'Famous last words' said Jack, still not convinced.

As it was nearing lunchtime by the time they got to the beach, they stopped off at Spiros' and bought some lunch, to save them coming back up, and some coffees to have once they had secured their sun beds.

'I think maybe you need umbrellas on the beach today' said Spiros to Elaine, pointing to the ever darkening sky, 'Maybe there is a big storm coming.'

'No Spiro, it's just a few clouds, it'll be fine. I was just saying to the others, they'll get burned off by the sun. You men worry too much.'

'OK, no problem then' said Spiros, 'you go to beach and have sunbathing. Everything will be good.'

'Spiro didn't look convinced that everything was going to be alright, did he' said Jack to Sid.

'No, he didn't, but it's okay, Michael Fish here reckons there is no storm so we'll be fine!'

The beach was pretty empty, bar a dozen or so occupied sun beds so they managed to get four beds together easily. As the sea was extremely rough they decided against their normal place at the front of the beach, choosing instead four beds at the back against the rocks. It was still hot but down there on the beach there was a wonderful breeze which seemed to knock the temperature down by around ten degrees.

As the sea was far too rough to go in swimming, the four friends got out their Kindles and iPods to amuse themselves. After eating the rolls they had bought earlier, they settled down for an afternoon snooze. Unfortunately Mother Nature had other ideas.

'I don't want to worry anyone but I really think it's time we went back to the hotel' shouted Jack to wake the others up.

'Oh what's the matter now Jack?' said Andrea, sitting up on the sun bed, 'Oh shit, I see what you mean.'

Out at sea, but not that far away, was a twister that looked like it was heading for shore. The sky was now completely black and the wind was really whipping up.

Sid and Elaine had now also woken up and after one look at what the weather was doing, agreed with Jack that they really needed to get off the beach. They quickly got dressed and grabbed their towels in record time and just as they started to walk along the beach the heavens opened. Luckily they weren't far from Spiros' van and managed to take shelter under his canopy while he was packing away his food.

'Look, what did I tell you' said Spiros as he hurriedly locked his van down, putting any perishables in the boot of his car. 'This is going to be a very big storm you need to get back to the hotel.'

'I told them, they should have listened to me' said Jack smugly, 'if it's okay with you Spiro, we can shelter here until it passes and then walk back.'

Spiros stopped what he was doing and stared at Jack in amazement.

'This is no problem but you may be here for some time, my friend, as the storm may last now until tomorrow. I really don't think you want to be out in it tonight. Wait until I have put the food away and I will drive you all back to the hotel.'

'Oh Spiro, you don't have to do that, we'll be fine. It's only a bit of rain; we're used to that where we come from!'

'My dear Andrea, I think it is a bit more than a bit of rain, have you seen over there?'

Everyone looked to where Spiros was pointing and saw that the road that they needed to walk down was almost flooded and water was pouring down it in torrents.

'Blimey, I didn't think it had got that bad. Perhaps we will take you up on that lift after all.'

'Right, I am ready, get in the car and put your seat belts on'

They all got in the car with Spiros and did as he said and put their seat belts on. It was barely a three minute drive to the hotel on a normal day but with the storm getting worse by the minute, it took them almost twenty minutes to drive along a road that had now turned into a raging river. Luckily Spiros' car was actually a four by four monster and handled the conditions well but even in a vehicle like this it turned out to be an extremely scary journey and they were all glad when they finally reached the hotel steps.

'Thank you so much for this Spiro, we really appreciate it' said Jack, unbuckling himself and grabbing the towels from the back shelf.

'No problem Jack, I must go now as I have animals to get in back at home. Hopefully I will see you again before you go home.'

'Flipping hell, I hope so. Surely this can't last until the end of the week. I've got some serious sunbathing to do.'

'No, I'm sure it won't. Now, get ready to run and be careful those steps will be very slippy with the rain.'

They said goodbye to Spiros and ran as fast as they could without slipping, up the steps into the hotel.

'Wow, that was scary' said Sid who had been sitting in the front with Spiros. 'Those window wipers were going nineteen to the dozen; I couldn't see a bloody thing. It's a good job Spiro knows that road as well as he does or we could have ended up in a ditch somewhere. And you' he said pointing at Jack, 'you wanted to walk back here.'

'Okay, perhaps that wasn't one of my better suggestions. Well at least we are back now, I have a feeling we won't be going very far this evening though. I hope the others managed to get back before the storm hit'

Jack was right, no-one did go very far that evening and once everyone had been accounted for, Jack took the liberty of booking a table for them all at the hotel. By the time everyone had showered and changed and got down to the bar, the storm was in full flow, complete with deafening cracks of thunder and lightning strikes that lit up the whole hotel. Christos and Anna had rallied the troops and set up additional tables where they could and Eleni and Lambros put out a limited selection menu to accommodate for all the extra mouths that needed feeding.

The noise in the bar was deafening as pretty much everyone in the hotel had congregated there. Christos and Petros started ferrying people over to the restaurant to their waiting tables whilst Anna was letting everyone left in the bar know what time they would be eventually seated. Jack's table for fourteen wouldn't be ready for at least another half hour or so, which suited everyone and they sat in the bar until they were called through by Christos.

While they were waiting with their drinks, Johnson arrived in the bar with Edison and Caroline following behind.

'Oh look what the cat's dragged in' said Mandy, pointing over to them. 'I didn't think he'd have the nerve to show his face after his little performance the other day. But then it wouldn't surprise me if he thought he'd done nothing wrong.'

'Right, you lot stay here; I'm going over there to have it out with my brother and that bastard son of his. Come on Andrea, I might need you to restrain me.'

The others watched as Jack, closely followed by Andrea, went marching over the other side of the bar where Edison and his family were currently sitting.

Caroline was the first up on her feet to greet them.

'Jackson. Andrea. How wonderful to see you both. How was your little break that your friends sent you on?'

'It was lovely Caroline. Very relaxing, thank you. Well it was until we got back here and found out what your darling son had been up to in our absence.'

'I'm sure I don't know what you mean Jackson. What on earth are you talking about?'

Johnson had gone a whiter shade of pale as Jack looked at him.

'Oh, I take it you haven't told Mummy and Daddy what you've been up to then?'

'For God's sake Johnson' said Edison, looking completely defeated, 'please don't tell me you're up to your old tricks again.'

'Well if his old tricks include slapping a barmaid because she wouldn't go out with him or trying to force himself onto Sophie, then yes he has.'

'No, I'm sorry Jackson' said Caroline, standing by the side of her son as if to protect him, 'but I'm afraid you are dreadfully wrong there. My Johnson would never do anything like that, would you darling?'

Johnson smirked, 'No Mummy, of course I wouldn't. What do you take me for? I told you before; these people have it in for me. They're just jealous of us because of what we have.'

'Jealous of you' spat Andrea, 'you must be joking. So basically you are saying that my daughter is a liar and Adam didn't catch you trying it on with her as she was coming out of her room.'

'Oh and the barmaid's brother and father came to the hotel and gave you a black eye just for the fun of it, did they?'

'So you didn't get mugged at all then' said Edison, shaking his head.

'Of course he did' argued Caroline, 'are you going to believe your own son or this pathetic attempt to discredit him by your, so called family. Johnson's right, they have always had it in for him. I don't know why we bothered coming here in the first place; we really don't fit in with all these ruffians.'

'You cheeky bitch, I'll show you what ruffians we are when I get hold of you.' Andrea lunged at Caroline, only to be pulled back by Jack.

'Right, stop it everyone. I'm sorry Johnson, I know you're my son but I just can't do this anymore.'

'Do what anymore, Edison, what do you mean?'

'Lie for your precious son, Caroline, that's what. You think he's all sweet and innocent, well I can assure you he's not. I have had to cover for him time and time again. Paying fines when the police have charged him for speeding and drug offences. Yes, the little darling didn't get bored with his college course; he was kicked off for selling drugs to his classmates. Then there was the hush money paid out to parents of girls that he had taken advantage of and who wanted to prosecute. He beat one poor girl up so badly that she ended up in hospital. I finally managed to stop her going to the police by paying for her to go through college. So, yes I believe Jackson and Andrea one hundred percent and I am mortified that a son of mine could stoop so low.'

Both Johnson and Caroline stood looking at Edison in total disbelief. Then Caroline turned to her son.

'Is this all true, Johnson?'

'What if it is, it's not like I killed anyone or anything. I don't know what all the fuss is; most of those girls were slags who deserved what they got.'

Caroline pulled her arm back and slapped her son with so much force that his feet left the ground.

'Get out of my sight, you disgusting animal. When we get back to England you can pack your things and move out. Where you go is no concern of mine but I can assure you that you will never set foot in my home again.'

Caroline then turned to her husband with tears running down her face.

'Why did you lie for all these years?'

'To protect you, my love. I knew how much you idolised the boy and if you had known what he was really like, it would have broken your heart, but unfortunately this time he has overstepped the mark and I really can't lie for him anymore.'

'I can't understand how he's turned out like this. I've always been there for him and I've never refused him anything. How could he repay me like this?'

'I think it's because you have always given him everything Caroline,' sighed Jack. 'He now thinks it's his God given right to have everything he wants and if it's not offered then he'll just take it anyway.'

'I think you could be right Jackson' said Caroline, who seemed to be deflating by the minute, 'I know it's too little, too late, but I really do apologise on behalf of wayward son. I honestly don't know why I used to listen to the poison he used to spew, mainly about you and Andrea by the way. Edison is right, I was totally blinded by him and in my eyes he could do no wrong. Well now I know the truth about him and I can assure you, things will change. Right, I don't know about you Edison, but I have completely lost my appetite. Shall we just go up to the room? I don't think I could face everyone now after everything.'

'Don't feel you have to hide away because of Johnson' said Andrea, actually feeling quite sorry for the woman now. 'I'm sure no-one is going to blame you'.

'No, you're right Caroline' said Edison, finishing his drink, 'I think we need some time alone to get our heads around what we do next, and I know Caroline has said it Jack, but we really do apologise for everything that little bastard has done over the years. Right hopefully we'll see you before we go but you'll understand now if we keep a bit of a low profile.'

Caroline and Edison made their way out of the bar and towards their room, leaving Andrea and Jack completely gobsmacked.

'Wow' said Jack, 'I'd heard rumours of things that boy had done but I wasn't sure if they were really true.'

'Well obviously they were' said Andrea, as she watched them leave the bar. 'I actually feel quite sorry for them, especially Caroline. To suddenly hear that your son, your pride and joy, is nothing more than a drug dealing pervert. It must be devastating.'

'Yeah I suppose it is. I do feel a bit guilt telling them but it had to be said. He couldn't keep going on the way he was or someone was going to get badly hurt and once he started on Sophie, well that was a line he should never have crossed. Right I suppose we'd better get back to the others and tell them what happened and hopefully we won't have to wait too long for our table.'

Andrea replayed the conversation that they had just had with Edison and Caroline while Jack got some drinks in. They all agreed that Johnson had got exactly what he deserved and that Jack shouldn't feel guilty about telling his brother and sister-in-law about his antics.

'I bet she doesn't think the sun shines out of his backside now, does she?' asked Sid. 'I know he's your nephew Jack, but the geezer needs a bloody good kicking if you ask me.'

'Oh believe me, I'd like nothing better than to give the little scroat a good hiding but unfortunately in this day and age you can't get away with things like

237

that anymore. Don't worry, being kicked out of the family home and stopping all his allowances will have much more of an impact on him than a kicking any day. The thought of having to work for a living and not being able to ponce off mummy and daddy must be killing him.'

'Right you two, stop rabbiting, our table's ready and we need to grab an umbrella and run across to the restaurant' said Elaine, rounding up the rest of them.

They did a relay run with the couple of big umbrellas that were available and managed to get to their table without getting too wet. The storm was still raging and the rain was coming down like stair rods. Lightening was flashing across the sky lighting up the whole resort and the thunder was so loud it sounded like a war zone.

'I haven't seen a storm like this in years' said Elaine, looking out to where the water was running like a river down the street, 'I think the last one like this was when we went to Ibiza. Do you remember Sid?'

'Flipping hell, that's going back a bit. What was it, twenty years ago? Where's that time gone, eh? It only seems like last year. That was a good holiday wasn't it?'

'Yeah, back in the days when we could go out and have a skin full every night and still manage to get up early for breakfast. I have a good drink now; it takes me a week to get over it!'

'Tell me about it' agreed Andrea, 'talking about a good drink, here's Lambros to take our drinks order.'

'Okay everyone, how are we all doing. Are you enjoying the storm?'

'It's fabulous Lambros' replied Sid, 'but I think I'd enjoy it a lot better with a large Mythos!'

'No problem Sid' laughed Lambros, 'Now let me sort your drinks out first and then I will come back to take your food order once you have looked at the menus. Just to let you know, we have no lamb or salmon left but pretty much everything else on the menu is still there, which isn't bad considering how many people we have served already this evening.'

'I think you've done brilliantly' said Andrea, 'I bet most of the hotels round here haven't gone out of their way like you have.'

'Well, that's why you all keep coming back every year' laughed Lambros, 'now let me go and get those drinks for you.'

They all ended up having a fabulous evening, with great food, and a spectacular light show going on, everyone had pretty much forgotten about the drama with Jack's family. After dinner they all ran the gauntlet back over to the hotel and sat in the bar drinking for a couple of hours. No-one really wanted an early night as there wasn't much chance of getting a lot of sleep with the storm still raging overhead. They eventually called it a day around one o'clock and surprisingly nearly everyone managed to get some sleep, despite the noise outside. That is apart from Lizzie who sat awake most of the night going through the last few days in her head and feeling very troubled.

Tuesday 16th September

After the horrific storms that battered the island the previous day, nobody thought that they would see the sun again before they went home but, as quickly as the rain came, it went and Tuesday morning dawned as if the apocalyptic style weather had all been just a bad dream.

'Can you believe this weather?' asked Elaine as she went out on the balcony.

'No, it's mental' said Sid in the middle of getting dressed, 'if you hadn't seen the weather yesterday with your own eyes, you wouldn't believe it had happened. There's not a trace of all that rain yesterday.'

'It's still a bit cloudy and I bet the beach has been battered, so perhaps we should give it a miss today.'

'Yeh, I think you're right babe. It's stopped raining but it's still not really sunbathing weather quite yet. Let's do something this morning and hopefully the sun will be out after lunch. What do you fancy doing?'

'Right don't laugh Sid, but have you seen those little train things that go around the resort? Well I fancy a trip on one of those. They do one up to Bohali which would be really nice. We could have a wander round and have a couple of drinks and then come back in time for lunch. I think it stops at a perfume factory as well.'

'Are you for real Laney? You expect me to sit on one of those little kiddie trains and go all the way to Zante Town and Bohali. I'll be the bloody laughing stock.'

'No you won't, I'm going to ask Jack and Andrea and some of the others too. It will be fun.'

'Yeh, course it will!'

'You're such a killjoy. Come on let's go and get some breakfast and see who else wants to join us on the Fun Train!'

Andrea and Jack were already tucking into their breakfast when they walked into the breakfast room.

Sid walked over to their table while Elaine got a couple of cups of coffee to bring over.

'Morning Andrea, Jack. You're both up early. I'm surprised you managed to sleep through that storm last night.'

'It was a bit loud' agreed Andrea, 'but we wacked the air conditioning up and the noise drowned out the bangs and crashes. How did you two sleep?'

'Like a bloody log' said Sid sitting down as Elaine put a black coffee in front of him, 'and I woke up feeling really refreshed and looking forward to the day ahead until this silly mare put the kibosh on it.'

'Oh gawd, what's she done now?' laughed Jack.

'Well, because it's still not quite sunbathing weather, dopey here thought it would be a good idea if we all got on one of those silly little train things that goes round the resort and up to Bohali.'

'That's a brilliant idea Laney' cried Andrea, 'I've always wanted to go on the train and it'll be nice to go up to Bohali and take in those views. We can ask a few of the others if they want to come and make an outing of it.'

'Bloody typical. I should have known you'd side with her. You two are going to make complete muppets out of us aren't you?'

''No love, nature's already beaten us to that' laughed Elaine. 'Oh look here comes Sophie, Mandy and the boys; let's ask them if they want to tag along and don't look like that Sid, you and Jack are coming with us, no arguments. It'll be fun.'

After a hearty breakfast Elaine and Sid, along with Andrea, Jack, Mandy, Sophie, Adam and Raymond, all left the hotel to catch the fun train into town and then onto Bohali which was in the hills overlooking Zante Town. Jamie and Stephen refused point blank to go and stayed round the pool reading and listening to music, together with Lizzie who decided that it would be too much for her back to cope with. No-one had seen Edison, Caroline or Johnson since Jack's outburst the previous evening.

They were to catch the train outside of Costa's Supermarket, which was about one hundred meters from the hotel on the main road and were met by a rather jolly Greek lady who sold them the tickets for their trip. Once all the tickets were purchased, they waited around ten minutes before Sid noticed the train slowly snaking its way down the main road towards them.

'Oh God, here it comes, the Noddy train. I can't believe you're making me go on this Elaine. Don't you dare take any photos because if any of the blokes down the pub see this, I'll never hear the last of it.'

'Get over yourself Sid, I'm sure they've all got better things to worry about than you going on a little train on your holidays. Now get on, shut up and enjoy yourself!'

'Come on Jack, back me up mate. I'm being bullied here.'

'I'm staying out of it' said Jack opening the little door to let Andrea on as the train stopped in front of them. 'I'd like to keep my manhood intact, thank you all the same!'

'Oh, stop moaning you pair of tarts' laughed Mandy, jumping on the train and sitting behind Andrea and Elaine, 'anyone would think you were going to be

245

publically flogged instead of going for a likkle ride on a choo choo train.'

'You will all pay for this' warned Sid as him and Jack finally got themselves on the train and sat down, 'me and Jack are grown men and will not be treated this way.'

'Yeh, whatever' said Elaine as the others doubled up with laughter and finally even Sid and Jack joined in with them.

The train finally got underway and, despite their protestations, the men started to really enjoy themselves. Sid got his phone out and started to video their journey down the main road out of Kalamaki while Jack took pictures of everyone as they were going along, whilst shouting "yassoo" to random people.

By the time the train pulled into Zante Town for its first stop, they were all having a great time, even Sid and Jack who finally admitted that it was a good idea of Elaine's to go on it and had somehow managed to get the whole train to singing along to their own version of "the wheels on the train go round and round", much to the joy of Elaine and

Andrea, who took great delight in filming the whole thing.

After it let a few passengers off in Zante Town, the fun train carried on out of town before it made a short stop at a small perfumery where they were shown how they made perfume and then handed round samples of the scents to try.

'Ooh, I quite like this one' said Elaine, shoving her wrist under Sid's note.

'It's not bad, but it's no Chanel No. 5 is it?'

'No I suppose not but it'd make a nice present for your sister'.

'Bloody hell Laney, for that price you could get some proper stuff at the airport.'

'Well, I like it, so I'm getting a bottle. It's a really lovely smell and it's nice to support these little independent companies'.

Both Elaine and Andrea bought a bottle each of the scent while Sid and Jack went to sit outside with the others to complain again, how they thought it was all a rip-off.

Once everyone was back on board, the train carried on winding its way up to Bohali, high above the city.

'Wow, look at that view' said Sophie to her mum as they rounded the bend to park. 'It reminds me a bit of where Dad lives in Italy.'

'I don't know love. When I was with your father we lived in a flat in a grotty area in Naples. It certainly didn't look like this.'

'He lives in Sorrento now, doesn't he Sophie?' asked Mandy.

'Yeh, him and his wife Maria live in a hilltop villa overlooking the Med. It's really beautiful.'

'Right, I think the first port of call has to be that little place over there' said Andrea pointing to a café with the most amazing view, 'because I don't know about you lot, but I'm absolutely gasping',

The eight of them found a table and ordered a selection of drinks. The owner brought out their order, complete with some bowls of crisps and nuts and they sat drinking and taking photos of the magnificent views of Zante Town, the port and the Ionian Sea that was sparkling in the sunshine.

'Bloody typical, that is' said Jack, 'the minute we come out because the weather's crap, the sun decides to show itself.'

'You just knew that would happen, but it is definitely getting hotter' agreed Andrea, 'I can feel it burning my arm as the shade is moving over'

Andrea was right, the sun had come out and it was starting to get very warm indeed.

'Right then, who's walking up to this castle with me? asked Adam, finishing his drink.

'I'll come with you' said Sophie getting up, 'anyone else up for it?'

'Oh go on then, I'll come with the pair of you' said Raymond putting on his cap and sunglasses.

'Sod that' said Andrea, 'I'm staying here, it's far too hot to go climbing hills.'

The others all agreed with Andrea and so it was left to Raymond to join Sophie and Adam on the walk up to the castle. Those that were left finished their drinks and then had a walk around the village, popping into the gift shop for a browse and then ending up in another bar further up where they ordered some dips, olives and chips to snack on while they had another drink as they could feel themselves dehydrating by the minute.

Before long, the others returned from the castle with Raymond looking incredibly hot and bothered.

'You could have warned us it was that steep. Or am I just getting old?' said Raymond flopping down next to Jack and ordering a large water.

'I think you're just getting old mate because those two don't seem to have broken sweat!'

Sophie and Adam were just behind Raymond and were chatting away to each other, looking no more exhausted than when they left.

'Oh to be young again' said Jack wistfully. 'It is nice that those two are getting on so well isn't it?'

'Yeh, they do seem to be getting a little bit close, don't they?' said Raymond glumly.

'You don't seem as if you are very happy about that Raymond.'

'No, I'm absolutely fine with it Jack. Take no notice, I'm just bushed.'

'Right it looks like the train is getting ready to get going back to Kalamaki, so we'd better get a move on' said Mandy, rounding everyone up.

'Oh just when I was getting comfortable again' said Raymond, dragging himself up to get back onto the train. 'I think I may have to have a little nap when we get back to the hotel.'

'I think I may join you' said Andrea, 'well obviously not literally, but I'm knackered as well and I haven't even done anything. I think it's this heat, it's so draining.'

They all trooped back onto the fun train and it wasn't long before it set off back down the hill into Zante Town. After picking up a couple of people there, it made its way past the harbour, out of the city and back to Kalamaki. The journey back took around thirty minutes but it seemed longer as the midday sun was now beating down on them relentlessly and by the time they got off the train and walked back to the hotel, even Sophie and Adam had started to flag.

'I don't know about you but I'm going up to change into my swim things and then go for a nice long dip' said Elaine, fanning herself with a flyer she had picked up along the way.

'That's the best idea you've come up with all holiday babes' said Sid, getting the room key out ready.

'Glad I'm of some use then' she laughed, 'right see you all back round the pool. First one down grab a few beds.'

Back in their air conditioned room Elaine and Sid had a quick wash and then laid on the bed to cool down a bit before changing into swimwear and putting on some factor thirty.

'Right, I feel a bit more human now' said Elaine putting her hair up in a clip. 'Let's go and knock on Andrea and Jack's door and see if they're ready yet. I don't know about you but a swim and a shandy are calling me.'

They got their towels and went to go out the door, only to find that Andrea and Jack had beaten them to it and were just about to knock for them. The four of them went down by the pool where Mandy had already got some sun beds ready for them. They laid their towels down, put the umbrellas up and then went and jumped in the pool.

'Oh God, that feels so good' said Andrea as she lay on her back in the cool water, 'sometimes I moan that this pool is too cold but today it feels amazing. I think I'll have a few minutes in here, go and get a drink and then maybe have forty winks under the umbrella.'

True to her word, Andrea got out of the pool, dried herself off and got some bottles of ice cold water to hand round. She then curled up on her sun bed and fell asleep. Before long nearly everyone had followed suit, apart from Raymond who had found Lizzie and gone back to their room for a sleep and Sophie and Adam who were still in the pool swimming.

At around two thirty everyone seemed to start stirring, mainly due to hunger. A few of them ambled over to the snack bar and got some lunch and then sat around the pool area reading or chatting.

'So what is everyone doing tonight then' asked Adam, 'only me and Soph thought we might take in a few bars down at Laganas.'

'Did someone mention Laganas?' said Jamie as he and Stephen walked through the pool area on their way back to the hotel.

'Hello boys, where have you been today?' asked Jack as his son came and plonked himself on his sun bed.

'Oh we thought we'd do a tour of the hotel pools in the area. We did have a wander down to the beach but the sea was so rough you couldn't really get on it. How did your little trip on the choo choo train go?'

'It was actually quite good. We went up to Bohali which was really beautiful. The views are amazing up there, you should have come.'

'No, you're alright Dad. We were quite happy staying here. So, who's going to Laganas tonight then?'

'Well me and Adam are definitely going' said Sophie, 'do you two want to tag along as well?'

'Yeah, I think we're up for that. Anyone else coming?'

'What's this Laganas place like then?' said Raymond, as he came back out to the pool with Lizzie to catch the last hour of sun.

'I honestly think you'd be better staying here with us Raymond' said Sid laughing.

'Why, what's wrong with it? I don't even know where it is.'

'It's the next resort down from here and it couldn't be any different from Kalamaki if it tried' said Sid, trying to explain what Laganas was like, 'let's put it this way, it's definitely more attracted to the youngsters. It's full of bars, fast food places, night clubs and strip joints and most of the kids staying there don't go out until we're ready to go to bed!'

'So, there you go dad, you're more than welcome to join us if you want.'

'No, I think I'll give it a miss Adam, thanks all the same. I think perhaps me and your mum might have a meal in that restaurant we all went to the night, Zorbas I think, wasn't it Sid?'

'That's right mate, it's a really nice restaurant. You won't go far wrong there. We normally go there on our last night. I think we're just going to walk and see what takes our fancy. I think Mandy said she was meeting some friends tonight so it'll just be the four of us.'

'I must admit I fancy trying that new restaurant down the old road. I saw it on Facebook and it's getting pretty good reviews' said Elaine.

'Oh, I know the one you're talking about' said Andrea getting out her phone, 'yeh here it is. Lemonia it's called and it is getting really good reviews. It looks quite nice doesn't it?'

'Looks like that's our evening sorted then Sid. I'm glad we made a good choice again' laughed Jack, as he took a whack on the head from Andrea's blow up pillow.

Leaving the youngsters to chat about their evening plans, Elaine and Sid, along with Andrea and Jack, took their leave and went up to their respective rooms to start getting ready for that evening, arranging to meet back up in the bar around seven thirty for the now obligatory cocktails. When they all got back down to the bar there was no sign of the others, who had all gone back to start getting ready.

'I must admit I'm not that happy about Sophie going into Laganas' said Andrea, looking worried, 'especially late at night, you hear so many stories.'

'Oh she'll be alright Andrea' said Jack, 'she's got three strapping lads with her. I'm sure she'll be well looked after, especially by young Adam who I think's got a soft spot for her.'

'I noticed that. They actually make a lovely couple, don't they?'

'I think so but I don't think Raymond did when I mentioned it earlier today. But to be fair he most probably thinks it will all end in heartache because of the distance between them.'

'Blimey, I hope she doesn't decide to go and live in Australia, I don't think I could handle that.'

'Andrea, they've only known each other a couple of days' laughed Elaine, 'she's hardly going to suddenly jet off to the other side of the world and leave her family, home and business is she?'

'No I suppose not, I'm just being silly aren't I? Right enough of Sophie and Adam, let's make a move down to this restaurant. I'm starving and I'm dying to find out what this place is like.'

The four of them walked down to the other end of the resort and found the restaurant straight away. The décor was beautifully done and it really stood out amongst the other restaurants near it. They went in hoping that the food was as classy as the furnishings.

A young waiter, with the personality of dishcloth, grabbed them before they had even stepped over the threshold and took them to a table near the toilets, even though there were plenty of seats at the front overlooking the resort. After telling the waiter at least three times that they weren't happy with the table and wanted one at the front of the restaurant, they were eventually moved to a table of their choosing. They sat down and started to look at the menus that were already on the table and no sooner had they opened them than the same waiter returned for their order.

'Flipping hell mate, I've only just opened the menu' said Sid, getting a bit annoyed now. 'Give us a chance to have a look can you?'

The waiter disappeared and they carried on looking at the menu. The food looked lovely; albeit a bit expensive but they all agreed that you do get what you pay for in this world. Once they had all decided what they wanted, Sid tried to attract the waiter's attention but to no avail. It took another ten minutes before the waiter came over to them and that was only to take down a drinks order.

'Bit bloody slow here aren't they' said Jack as they sat waiting, seemingly forever, for their drinks.

'Yeh' agreed Sid, 'couldn't wait to drag us in the place and now they've got us in they've buggered off.'

Their drinks finally arrived and the food was eventually ordered but it was then another fifteen minutes or so before their starters arrived. The food was beautifully presented and tasty but cold.

'Any other place and I'd send this back' said Andrea, 'but I'm too hungry to wait another half an hour for it to be brought out again.'

'Luckily mine is meant to be cold' said Jack, tucking into chicken liver pate, 'but I don't envy you two with your soup.'

'No, it's stone cold' said Elaine, 'but as Andrea said, if we send it back we'll probably have to wait an eternity for it to be heated up and I can't be bothered. I will tell him when he comes and gets the dishes though.'

They didn't have to wait long for the dishes to be collected as the waiter grabbed them almost before Jack had put his knife down.

'I know you can't do anything about it now' said Andrea to the waiter before he made off with their plates, 'but I just thought we'd let you know that both the soups were cold.'

'Okay, I'll tell Chef' said the waiter before scurrying off again.

'Oh, nice to get an apology then' said Andrea, 'not exactly big on customer service are they? Let's just hope the main courses are better.'

Unfortunately they never got to find out if they were because, after yet another twenty minutes wait, the waiter came up again to inform them that they had run out of chicken, which was what Elaine and Jack had ordered.

'Actually mate' said Sid, getting really annoyed now. 'why don't you just forget the main courses. Tell us how much we owe you for the starters and the drinks and we'll leave it there.'

'Okay, no problem I'll get the bill'

'Unbelievable, they're not even trying to keep us here. They obviously don't want the custom. Why have they only just realised they've run out of chicken? Didn't they realise that when they took our order. Bloody useless'

'Well I can assure them that they won't be getting my custom again' said Jack, getting some money out to pay, 'and they won't be getting a tip.'

They paid the bill for the small amount of food and drink that they had left the restaurant.

'Well it's a bit late to go to another restaurant now' said Sid, 'so who fancies slumming it and getting a dirty great burger?'

They all took Sid up on his idea and walked down the road to the fast food outlet that always seemed to be filled with locals and tourists alike. They sat in and got served straight away, all ordering burgers, chips and beers.

'Oh my God' said Elaine with her mouth full, 'this is the best burger I've ever tasted. It is so good. I'm actually glad that restaurant was crap otherwise I'd never have got to try this.'

Everyone agreed that the food was indeed delicious and they were all completely stuffed once they had finished everything that had been brought out.

'I couldn't eat another thing' said Jack, holding his stomach, 'I'm done in, I think I need a walk now before I explode.'

They paid the bill, which was actually less than the paltry amount that they'd had in Limonaria, and started walking back to the hotel.

Everyone was still full up by the time they got back so even a night cap was out of the question. They all decided that an early night wouldn't hurt anyway, especially after the late night they'd had the previous night because of the storms, so said their goodnights and made their way up to their rooms.

Wednesday 17th September

Elaine and Sid were woken the next morning to the sound of voices outside their room.

'Sid, wake up' said Elaine shaking him. 'That sounds like Andrea and Sophie outside. Put something on and go and see what they are up to.'

'Really, what's the time and why can't you go?'

'It's half past seven, so we'd be getting up in a little bit anyway. I can't go to the door like this, my hair's all over the place. Stop moaning and go and find out what's happening.'

Sid put on a t-shirt and some shorts and opened the door while Elaine smoothed her hair down and hunted down something to cover herself with. Sophie was staying in the room a couple of doors along from Elaine and Sid's and when he opened the door he found her and Andrea standing in the corridor looking quite upset. Sophie was still in the clothes that she went out in the previous evening and looked quite dishevelled.

'Morning ladies, what's going on' asked Sid.

'Oh hello Sid' said Andrea, 'sorry we didn't wake you and Elaine up did we?'

'No, we was just getting up anyway' said Elaine appearing in the doorway with her dressing gown on. 'What's happened? You look like you've been up all night Soph!'

'I told you I was uneasy about them going into Laganas didn't I. Poor old Adam ended up in hospital last night.'

Elaine looked completely shocked. 'No way. Is he OK?'

'Yeh, luckily he only had a couple of stitches in his hand and over his eye and a few bruises. Sophie says she was up the hospital with him all night. They've only just got back. Adam's back in his room sleeping now.'

'Oh my God, what happened to him?'

'He got beaten up Elaine. Some bloke was trying it on with me in a bar and just wouldn't take no for an answer. Adam stepped in and told him to leave me alone and we thought nothing more of it.

Unfortunately the bloke seemed to hold a grudge and when we left the bar a couple of hours later, him and a couple of his mates were waiting for us and laid into Adam, really roughing him up. The owner of the bar saw what happened, brought us back inside and called the police. Luckily he knew who the guy was and told the police that it was a completely unprovoked attack. He then got one of his staff to run us to the hospital where we spent the rest of the night.

'What a nightmare' said Sid, 'are you alright? And what about Jamie and Stephen?

'I'm fine, just knackered. Jamie and Stephen called it a night about an hour before it all happened, so they are most probably still in bed blissfully unaware of what happened. I just wish we'd left when they did and then Adam wouldn't be black and blue. But, there you go, not much we can do about it now. I think I'll have a shower now and go straight to bed. I might catch up with you all round the pool this afternoon. Oh, and can you let Lizzie and Raymond know. Adam didn't want to call and worry them and by the time we got back all he wanted to do was sleep. I know they sometimes get up early and go for a walk so they might not be in their room'

'No problem, we'll just finish getting dressed and go down to breakfast. I'm sure we'll catch them down there and we can let them know what's happened.'

'You get some sleep sweetheart and we'll see you later on.'

Andrea hugged her daughter and then went back to her room to get Jack who was getting dressed. They all met up again ten minutes later outside the breakfast room.

'Oh look, here comes Lizzie and Raymond now round the pool' said Elaine, waving them over, 'they've obviously been for a walk down to the beach.'

'Morning everyone' said Lizzie, 'I must admit we didn't expect a welcoming committee when we got back. Okay what's happened, you all look very serious.'

Andrea suggested they all sit down in the empty lounge area outside the breakfast room and she filled them in on what had happened the previous evening.

Both Lizzie and Raymond were mortified when they were told about Adam and immediately wanted to go and see him. Jack suggested that they give it a couple of hours as he was most probably out for the count and they agreed with him that they would go and knock on his door around mid-morning.

'So, were Jamie and Stephen not with them then' asked Lizzie, 'only I thought they all went out together last night?'

'Yeh, they did' agreed Andrea, 'but according to Sophie they left about an hour before it all happened.'

'Why on earth didn't they come back with them then?'

'Who knows Lizzie? I suppose they wanted to spend some time together. They have been getting quite close. Or perhaps they were just enjoying themselves too much to leave with the boys. I had a bad feeling about this from the start. We should have stopped them going there and got them to come out with us instead.'

'I understand where you're coming from Andrea' said Jack, 'but at the end of the day they are both adults and I don't think either of them would have taken kindly to being told where they can go. I know Sophie certainly wouldn't and Adam seems as headstrong as her. In fact they are very much alike those two.'

'I know and we do have to be thankful if wasn't a lot worse.'

'You're absolutely right Andrea' agreed Raymond, 'you hear about so many of these kids carrying knives and all sorts. A black eye and a couple of stitches is nothing in comparison. In fact he's had worse than that falling off his surf board so I'm sure he'll be fine. Now, let's go and get some breakfast before I need hospital treatment for starvation.'

'You and me both' said Jack, 'I'll have something to eat and then I suppose I'd better go and say goodbye to my brother as they leave this morning.'

'Good riddance to bad rubbish is what I say' said Andrea

'I make you right love, but he is my brother after all and I think they were both mortified over what their darling son has been up to. I'm just going to see them off, which is the least I can do I suppose seeing as they came all this way for the wedding.'

'I suppose you're right, you can't really blame them for what Johnson does can you. I'll come with you to say goodbye after I've had some grub and at least ten cups of coffee!'

They went and sat down in the breakfast room, meeting up with Mandy, Jamie and Stephen who were promptly filled in with what happened to Adam. After breakfast the boys went to the beach, while Lizzie and Raymond went and sat round the pool, waiting until they could go and see how Adam was.

Andrea and Jack went outside to wave goodbye to Edison and Caroline, while Elaine and Sid went back up to their room to change into their swimwear and put on some sun tan lotion.

'Blimey, it all happens here, doesn't it?' said Sid as he rubbed sun cream into Elaine's back.

'I know, it's turning into a soap opera. You couldn't make it up, could you?'

'Well we've still got another two days left so there's plenty of time for more excitement.'

'Well let's hope it doesn't involve anyone else getting hurt. I can't believe we've only got two days left. You wait all year for it and then it's gone in a flash. It has been a good holiday though, hasn't it?'

'Yeh, it has. I hope Andrea and Jack have enjoyed it as much as we have. It must have been lovely then having all the family around them.'

'Well apart from Johnson that is.'

'Goes without saying babe. Right let's get round that pool and cram as much sunbathing as we can into our last couple of days. As it's our last day tomorrow, I think we should spend it on the beach. It'll be the last time we see the sea for a few months.'

'Sounds good to me. I'd have preferred to have gone down there today as I like spending my last

271

day round the pool but I'm sure Andrea will want to stay near to Sophie after what happened.'

'Oh, I forgot, Sophie and the boys go home tomorrow don't they. We are starting to go down in numbers now, aren't we? Here come Andrea and Jack now.'

'Right Sophie's okay and is sleeping and we've said our goodbyes to Edison and Caroline and it's still only 10 o'clock' said Andrea. 'We might as well go down to the beach for a few hours, unless you want to stay by the pool that is.'

'No, we were only just talking about that, weren't we Sid? I'd much prefer to spend tomorrow by the pool so I can nip up to the room to do odd bits of packing, You know what I'm like, so yes, we'd love to go to the beach today and it's still quite early so we'll have no problems getting a sun bed. You two can always have another day at the beach when we've gone.'

'No I doubt we will actually' said Andrea, 'we've only got one more day after you so we'll probably spend it round the pool or doing some shopping in town. Right let's get down that beach.'

They grabbed their towels off the beds round the pool and walked down to the beach one last time. After ordering some bowls of pasta salad for lunch from Spiros, they made their way down the walkway and found four sun beds right away in almost their usual spot. After putting their towels down and paying for the beds they went into the sea, which was like a millpond and as warm as bath water. They stayed in there for around an hour and then spent the rest of the morning sunbathing whilst reading or listening to music. Sid pulled the short straw and went and got their lunch around one ish and they sat around chatting while eating.

'So where shall we go on Sophie and the boy's last night then' asked Jack, 'I don't know about you but I thought perhaps all of us could go for a meal in Zante Town.'

'That's a really good idea Jack' agreed Andrea, 'I'd definitely be up for that. Any particular restaurant?'

'Well, there's that one just off the main square that does the Greek singing. The foods really good in there and it's pretty reasonable.'

'You mean Avalon don't you? asked Elaine, 'I like it in there, it's got a really good atmosphere and you're right the foods not bad either. We could go for a drink in the Hotel Panama after; they've got a bar on the roof which is really nice.'

'Yeh, we went up to the roof bar when we stayed there after the wedding' said Andrea, 'the views are fabulous. Blimey, that seems ages ago now. We're almost like an old married couple now, Jack.'

'You've had it now mate' laughed Sid as he ribbed Jack, 'once she gets you home it'll be DIY night and day, you'll lose ownership of the remote control and Saturdays will be spend trolling round endless shops. I do feel for you, I really do'

'What'd mean when I get home, that sounds like my life now!'

'Cheeky bugger' laughed Andrea, 'right that's going to cost you. What do you reckon Elaine, a bottle of Prosecco?'

'Oh at least. I'd make it two if I were you and some perfume at the airport!'

'See what I mean' laughed Sid.

The four friends spent the rest of the afternoon alternating between the sun beds and the sea before finally drying off around four thirty to make their way back to the hotel. Before they walked back they said their goodbyes to Spiros, promising to be back again next year and thanking him again for getting them back to the hotel safe and sound on the night of the storm.

When they got back to the hotel Jack went and asked Lizzie and Raymond if they fancied joining them in Zante Town for a meal that evening, which they were more than happy to do. He also found Jamie and Stephen who were also up for a night in town. When he got back to the room, Sophie was there with Adam who, apart from a black eye and a bandaged hand, didn't look too worse for wear. Andrea had already asked them if they fancied going out with them all and they were also happy to go. The only one left to ask was Mandy who, as per normal, was no-where to be found.

'Right, we'd better go and get our glad rags on if we're out with the olds tonight' said Sophie ushering Adam out the door.

'Excuse me young lady, less of the old. You're not too big to be put over my knee. Now are you sure you are okay to be going out tonight Adam?'

'Honestly Andrea, I'm absolutely fine. A bit sore but I've had worse coming off my surf board.'

'Yeh, that's what your dad said this morning. Right, shall we all meet down in the bar around seven o'clock. I'll phone down and ask Petros to call a couple of taxis for around half seven. Oh and if you see your Auntie Mandy, let her know what the plans are for this evening.'

Sophie and Adam left to get ready and then they all met back in the bar as planned. Surprisingly, Mandy was already sitting at the bar waiting for them all to arrive and even got a round of drinks in as everyone turned up. The taxis turned up dead on time and took them into Zante town in a convoy, dropping them off at the harbour.

As it was a lovely evening, they walked along the front chatting and taking photos. Everyone was in a great mood apart from, it seemed, Lizzie who had a face like thunder.

'Lizzie, what on earth is a matter' asked Andrea, 'you don't look at all happy? I hope it's nothing we've done. We haven't offended you in any way, have we?'

'No, no, nothing like that. I'm sorry, I'm just in a bit of pain with my arthritis and I suppose it's the thought of having to go back to England in a few days.'

'It is quite depressing knowing you've got to leave all this and go home. But we've had a fabulous time and it's been great having all you lot out here with us. We honestly couldn't have asked for a better wedding than we had, could we Jack.'

'No we couldn't, it's been a great couple of weeks, even if there were a few spanners thrown into the works!'

'I must admit it's never a dull moment when you come on holiday with us. Right, the restaurant is just round the corner. I've booked it for half eight so we got time for a couple of drinks. Any preferences to bars?'

'Well, this one here's supposed to be really good, if everyone's okay with it?' said Sid, starting to walk into the bar ahead of everyone else.

'It's fine by us' agreed Sophie and Adam.

They followed Sid in, got seated and ordered a round of drinks. It was very quiet in the bar, with maybe only another three or four people other than themselves in there, and the atmosphere was non-existent.

'What on earth made you want to come in here' asked Elaine, suddenly realising why both Sid and Jack made a beeline for that particular bar, 'Oh, I can see now, there's a bloody great telly up there with the football on. You must think we're stupid. Well we won't be staying in here long, so make the most of it.'

'Okay, sweetheart, anything you say' said Sid, bowing down to her. 'We only wanted to see if we've bought anyone because the transfer deadline is tomorrow.'

'Of course it is' said Andrea, slapping her palm against her head, 'we should have known, shouldn't we Elaine?'

'Absolutely' agreed Elaine, 'I was only wondering this morning if we had bought anyone yet.'

'Oh very funny. Think you're clever don't you?'

They all stayed for one drink, which was enough time for Sid and Jack to find out that Tottenham had still bought no new players, which then sparked another debate on football that Elaine and Andrea stayed well out of, having absolutely no interest in Harry Kane, Mousa Dembele or anyone else in the Spurs line up.

As they were still a bit early for their table booking, they took the scenic route round to the restaurant and got there just on time, as it was slowly starting to fill up. After being seated and ordering a round of drinks they sat and perused the menus, which weren't big as the restaurant didn't serve fancy or foreign cuisine, just fresh and authentic Greek food.

Once the food was brought up, everyone tucked in and commented on how good it was. After finishing the main courses, bowls of fresh fruit and plates of baklava were brought up, along with more drinks.

Elaine got up to use the ladies and Andrea jumped up to follow her. Once away from the tables, Andrea called Elaine over to whisper to her.

'Is it me, or have you noticed that Lizzie is knocking the drinks back?'

'Yeh, now you say it Andrea, she has had a few, which is weird because she normally only has a couple of drinks all night.'

'She hasn't been right for the last couple of days and I'm really not buying the excuse that her arthritis is playing up, there's definitely something wrong. I hope there's not a problem with her and Raymond. Well, I'm sure if she wants to talk about it, she will. Right let me have a quick wee and we'll get back to the others.'

Once everyone had finished, they paid the bill and then made their way to the roof top bar of the Panorama Hotel. They pretty much had the place to themselves, apart from a couple sitting at the bar and another group of around six people sitting at the other end. After ordering from the drinks menu, they all sat chatting about the holiday and generally chilling out. Apart from Lizzie, that is, who after having a large whisky then proceeding to order the strongest cocktail on the menu.

'Bloody hell' whispered Andrea to Elaine, 'have you seen Lizzie, she's getting absolutely blotto!'

'I know. She's really knocking them back. She'll pass out in a minute if she's not careful and, I don't know if you noticed, but she hasn't taken her eyes off Sophie and Adam.'

'I must admit I did notice that earlier on. She's definitely acting weird.'

'Right I don't know about everyone else,' said Jamie standing up, 'but me and Stephen are going to make our way back to the hotel.'

'Oh God, you're going home tomorrow aren't you' said Jack.

'Yeh, so am I unfortunately' said Sophie finishing her drink, 'so I suppose I'd better start making my way back as well. Nothing worse than a hangover at the airport.'

'I can't believe you're going home tomorrow' said Adam, looking crestfallen.

'No, neither can I' agreed Sophie, looking equally as upset. 'I'll really miss you.'

'Oh sweetheart, don't get upset, we can still stay in contact and perhaps you can come to Oz or I can come to England.' Adam went to put his arms round Sophie to give her a cuddle when Lizzie barged into them.

'Get away from her, just get away and leave her alone. You can't do this.'

'For God's sake mum, what's the problem with you tonight; we're only having a cuddle. What is it with Sophie that you can't handle?'

'The fact that she's your sister.'

Everyone went deathly quiet and stared at Lizzie.

'Lizzie, what did you just say?' said Andrea, looking totally confused. 'How can Sophie be Adam's sister? Unless…'

'I'm so sorry Andrea' cried Lizzie, 'I swear it was just the once. I never intended to get pregnant. Oh God, why did they have to hit it off so well? If they hadn't, no-one would have been any the wiser and it could have stayed my secret.'

Everyone just sat dumbfounded at Lizzie's outburst apart from Raymond who sat Lizzie down and put his arm around her.

'The trouble is Lizzie love; it never was just your secret. I've known about it all the time.' said Raymond.

'Hang on a minute' said Adam, looking as if his world had just caved in, 'so you are basically saying that not only are you not my dad, but that you've always known about it. Why the bloody hell didn't you let me in on this. I can't believe you've both kept this from me all my life. Was you ever going to tell me or was it just because you thought me and Sophie were getting too close for comfort. Shit, I can't handle this, I'm going for a walk on my own, I'll see you all back at the hotel.'

Adam got up and walked off. Sophie went to go with him but Andrea stopped her.

'No love, let him go, you can talk to him later when he's calmed down a bit. Right Lizzie, I think what you need to do is get some coffee down you and we'll all go back to the hotel as planned and then you can sit down and tell me everything, I think that's the least you can do.'

While they waited for their cabs, Lizzie went to the loo and washed her face, downed a couple of black coffees and then sat in the cab sipping a bottle of water. By the time they all got back to the hotel, she was almost sober. Jamie and Stephen made their excuses and went back to their room to finish packing for the morning and Mandy said she would leave them to it as no doubt she would hear all about it the next morning.

'I think we'll leave you to it as well Andrea' said Elaine, 'this is family business and you don't want us sitting there while your past is dragged up.'

'You're going nowhere' said Andrea, 'I need some moral support here, plus you are both our best friends, which in my book is as good as family. Go and grab some seats and get some coffees in for everyone. I'm just going to spend a penny.'

They found a table at the back of the bar. Luckily it was a quiet night as there were a lot of guests going home the next morning. Elaine ordered some coffees and some brandies to go with them and they sat back and waited for Andrea to return from the ladies. Once they were all seated, Lizzie tentatively gave her version of what had happened.

'Right, what can I say? I'm not proud of what I did or proud of the reasons why I did it. All I can say in my defence was that I was young and didn't know better.'

'We were both young Lizzie, but I would never have done what you did.'

'Yeh, I know and I've said I'm not proud of what I did.'

'Anyway, back then you were the only real good friend I had and when we went on holiday and you met Carlo, I admit I was jealous of both of you. I was jealous of you because Carlo was gorgeous and blokes like that never looked twice at me and jealous of Carlo because he was moving in on my friendship.

When you fell pregnant with Sophie, if you remember, I suggested that you get an abortion. I did it because I thought Carlo was going to take you away and I would lose you as a friend. Ironic isn't it? So, once you went back out to Italy to be with Carlo, that's when I started to really resent you because, by then, I started to have feelings for Carlo and had secretly hoped your relationship would amount to nothing so I could step in.'

Lizzie stopped talking to drink her coffee and to let what she had just said sink in before carrying on.

'Anyway, as you know, while you were in Italy, I met and married Raymond He was just starting to build up his business back then and he used to work really long hours and often be away for days at a time. I became bored and resentful, so when you and Carlo came back to live in England, I pretty much stopped at nothing to snare him.

After I made amends with you both and started seeing you all again regularly, I starting working my magic on Carlo who, even though he loved you, at the end of the day he was a hot bloodied Italian and he soon had his head turned by a busty blonde like I was back in the day. After I had his interest, the rest was easy. I lured him round my house one evening when Raymond was away, plied him with wine and finally my way with him. It only happened the once and afterwards Carlo was guilt ridden and told me that it could never happen again and to leave him and his family alone. To be fair he wasn't the only one who was guilt ridden. I felt terrible at what I had done to both Raymond and to you, Andrea.

I thought that I would eventually forget about what had happened and put it behind me but unfortunately a few weeks later, I found out that I was pregnant and it was obviously Carlo's. As neither of us wanted anything to do with the other, and to save everyone from hurt, I never told him and instead passed the baby off as Raymond's thinking no-one would be any the wiser! To save any future questions or awkwardness, I even talked Raymond into moving to Australia, where we stayed building a very successful life together with our son Adam.

So now you know the whole sordid story and why I started freaking out when Sophie and Adam started to get a bit close to each other!'

287

'I have to know Lizzie' said Raymond, looking like the wind had been knocked out of his sails, 'did you ever love me or was I just someone who could provide for you and Adam?'

'No, of course I loved you Raymond, you were always the only one for me, I was just infatuated with Carlo and once the deed was done it all fizzled out. Anyway, you said earlier that you have always known that Adam wasn't yours, but how?'

'Well, you're not the only one to have kept a secret all these years. I had mumps when I was a youngster and was told that the chances of ever fathering a child were pretty slim. When we first got together you showed no signs of ever wanting a child so the subject never really came up. I thought that if, at any time in the future you decided you did want to start a family then I would have some tests to see if there was anything that could be done. Anyway when you fell pregnant, I was pretty sure it wasn't mine but had some tests done anyway. They all came back showing I had a nil sperm count so I knew for certain that I couldn't be the father. I guessed it was Carlo when you suddenly didn't want to be around him or Andrea. I didn't know

288

whether or not you had feelings for Carlo and, as I was desperate not to lose you, I kept quiet about what I knew. When you suggested making a new start in Australia, I jumped at it and when Adam was born I forgot all about you cheating as I fell in love with him instantly. In my eyes he will always be my son.'

'Why didn't you say anything to me? Why keep it to yourself all this time?' said Lizzie, tears running down her face.

'Believe me, I was going to. I got very near to doing it a couple of times but I just couldn't do it. Why stir the past up when all it would bring would be heartbreak. If I'd have known it would all end like this, I would definitely have said something beforehand. Anyway, enough about me, I think it's Andrea and Sophie you need to be apologising to as well.'

Both Andrea and Sophie had sat through the whole revelation completely gobsmacked and in shock. Neither of them had been able to speak as they were trying to get their heads round what Lizzie had just sprung on them. Andrea suddenly got up and walked over to Lizzie, slapping her so hard across her face that she left a red hand print on her cheek.

'That's for being a complete bitch and sleeping with my husband while all the time trying be my best friend. I can't believe you did it but, knowing Carlo, I imagine he didn't put up a great deal of a fight. I always thought that he had cheated on me but I always thought it was with one of the waitresses in his restaurant. Maybe he slept with her as well, who knows. Perhaps Sophie has more brothers and sisters. To be honest, we were on the slippery slope to our marriage breaking up by then anyway but it's still no excuse.'

Lizzie said nothing. She just sat there holding her cheek, silently crying and looking completely ashamed of herself.

'Now, I could scream, shout, throw glasses at you or batter you within inches of your life' continued Andrea, sitting back down, 'but what good would it do. In my eyes, you've been punished enough by having to live with this all your life. Lying to your husband and son and giving up seeing your friends and family in the UK. You've also now got the horrendous task of explaining everything to Adam and just hoping that he'll understand that everything you did, you did for him. I certainly don't envy you that. But, you also proved you do have a heart by spilling the beans, regardless of the outcome, when you thought that Adam was getting too close to Sophie. So, although I don't forgive you for what you did to me, I think you've suffered enough and I'm willing to let bygones be bygones and put this back where it belongs, in the past.'

Lizzie looked at Andrea and through her tears thanked her friend for her understanding and compassion.

'Thank you Andrea. I swear to God you'll never know how much I regret doing what I did and how much it has eaten me up over the years. If I could go back in time..'

'Yes, but then you wouldn't have Adam.'

'True. Sophie, you've sat there very quietly. I'm sure you must hate me for what I've put you through. I know you were starting to get very close to Adam and I'm so very sorry for all of this.'

'I know I should hate you for what you did to my mum, but if she can get past it then so can I. It's funny really, you're right, me and Adam have got really close but not in the way you think. I think the world of him and he thinks the world of me but in a completely platonic way. We chatted about this the other night and we both said that it feels like we've known each other all our lives and we felt like we should be brother and sister. How weird is that, it's like we had some sort of connection. Anyway, I'm absolutely over the moon that he is actually my brother and I'm sure when he gets over the shock and calms down, he will be thrilled as well. Adam's probably more upset that you never told him more than anything.'

'You're right, I am. You couldn't have said that better if you tried Soph. I am over the moon that you're my sister but you should have told me mum'

Adam appeared in the bar after getting a cab back from Zante Town. His face was puffy and he had obviously been crying.

'Adam, sweetheart. I am so, so sorry you had to be told like this.'

292

Lizzie got up to hug her son but he moved away from her.

'Not yet mum, I think we've got a bit of talking to do, don't you?'

'Right, I think the three of us should go back to our room and see if we can't sort ourselves out' said Raymond getting up and bidding everyone goodnight.

The others watched the three of them walk back to their room to what would probably be a long night of talking.

'Bloody hell, I never saw that coming' said Elaine, still in shock over the revelations, 'right, if anyone else has got any earth shattering news, let's get it out in the open now!'

'Don't even joke about that Laney' said Sid looking worried, 'this holiday is throwing up more skeletons than an archaeological dig. We certainly don't need anymore. Now, I don't know about you but I'm knackered and I'd like to get a full day's sun on our last day, so I suggest we all hit the sack.'

They all agreed and made their way up to their rooms, some getting a better nights' sleep than others.

Thursday 18th September

'Oh no, I can't believe it's our last day' said Elaine as she awoke to Sid making a cup of tea.

'No, neither can I babes. I also can't believe what happened last night. Who'd have thought Lizzie was hiding that sort of secret.'

'Oh God, I know, poor old Andrea. That was such a shock. You were right what you said last night about skeletons coming out of the cupboard. Andrea and Jack have certainly had their fair share of them this holiday haven't they? What with Veronica being Jack's ex-wife and now Sophie finding out she has a secret brother. It's been like a bloody soap opera. I honestly think you could write a book about the last two weeks!'

'Yeh, I think you're right babe' agreed Sid, taking their mugs of tea out the balcony. 'well at least it looks like our last day is going to be a scorcher. There's not a cloud in the sky.'

'Perfect' said Elaine, taking in the beautiful vista before her, 'I'm going to miss this place when we leave tomorrow. But at least we know we've got it all to look forward to again next year'

'Yeh, but perhaps without all the drama! Anyway, we've not left yet so get that tea down you and let's get to breakfast. Don't forget that Sophie and the boys are going this morning and we don't want to miss seeing them off.'

Elaine and Sid finished their tea, had a quick wash, got dressed and made their way down to the breakfast room. As it was still quite early they were the only ones in there but they had no sooner sat down with some coffee and fruit juice when Andrea and Jack appeared. Close on their heels was Sophie, Jamie and Stephen, with Mandy bringing up the rear.

'So are you three all packed and ready to go home then' asked Sid.

'Yep, our bags are ready to go down but I'm not sure we're ready to go home yet' said Stephen. 'I really have had a fabulous holiday with you guys. I'll admit it now but when Jamie said his dad was getting married out here and the family were invited, I was very tempted to make some excuse up and not come. You hear so many horror stories about wedding parties abroad falling out but I have to admit, even with everything that's happened, you all just seem to take it in your stride and get on with having a good time. I really do have to take my hat off to you all.'

'Thanks for that Stephen' said Jack, 'I really appreciate it. It's nice to know that we are seen as a tight knit unit, and at the end of the day, nothing or no-one spoils our holiday. I'll let you know if we have any more dramas before we go home!'

Elaine, Sid and Mandy went and sorted out some sun beds round the pool while Andrea and Jack helped Sophie and the boys downstairs with their bags. They still had around an hour before the taxi turned up to take them to the airport so they all sat in the pool bar with coffees chatting until it was time for them to go.

'So have you managed to see Adam this morning?' asked Mandy as Sophie came and sat down next to her.

'I saw him first thing before breakfast. He'd been up half the night with his mum and dad, chatting in their room. He looked shattered but I think they've sorted everything out. It's going to be a bit weird for a while but I'm sure they'll be okay. Adam said he'll come and visit me when they go back to the UK next week.'

'Oh, they're not going back to Oz then?'

'No, they're staying at Lizzie's parents place for a few weeks. Adam said that his grandparents are in a home and are fading fast so understandably Lizzie wants to be there for them. It'll be good as I can get to know my kid brother a bit better and show him the sights. I think he's only ever been to England once and that was when he was very small and he came back for a few days with Raymond to sort some business out.'

'So, is he coming down to see you off this morning?' asked Andrea.

'No, I told him not to bother and go back to bed as he looked shattered. Lizzie actually rang me this morning to say have a safe journey and to apologise again. I asked them all to come to the restaurant when we get back and we can sit and have a proper chat then. I think she feels too ashamed to show her face this morning.'

'She needn't feel like that. Okay it was a shock at first but I've been thinking about it and these things happen for a reason. If she hadn't had Adam with your father then she most probably wouldn't have had children or it could have split her and Raymond up or me and your father could have carried on plodding along in a loveless relationship and I would never have met Jack. So I think it all turned out for the best, don't you?'

'Yeh, you're right mum. I wish everyone could be as understanding as you. The world would be a better place if they were. Right, I think that's our taxi just pulled in.'

Elaine, Sid and Mandy came up from the pool area to say their goodbyes and they all went through to reception where Sophie and the boys collected their luggage and loaded up the waiting taxi. After lots of hugs, kisses and tears, they finally drove off to the airport, leaving Andrea and Jack frantically waving until the taxi could no longer be seen.

'Andrea, what on earth are you crying for?' asked Elaine as they walked back to the pool, 'you'll be seeing them all again in a couple of days' time.'

'I know. I'm just being silly and I hate goodbyes.'

'Well I hope you get suitably upset when we drive off tomorrow' laughed Sid.

'Ah about that' said Jack. 'We were going to wait until the morning but I know Andrea won't be able to contain herself. We've changed our flights and are coming home with you on your flight tomorrow now.'

'No way' cried Elaine, 'you had an extra day booked. Why did you change it?'

'Well, we thought, what with all the palaver of last night that it might be a bit awkward if it was just us and Lizzie and Raymond left so we looked at the flights last night and as it only cost a few quid to change it we thought it would be nice to all travel home together. We were lucky though as there were only four seats left, so we only just made it.'

'Oh, that will be really lovely all going home together Andrea' said Elaine moving her sun lounger so it was in full sun. 'Right, last day, let's see if we can lay in it all day.'

'No problem' said Andrea who was applying her last day low factor oil, 'by the way, anyone seen Mandy? I'm sure she was here earlier but she seems to have disappeared again. I honestly don't know what my sister gets up to half the time. I must admit I thought she was going to be a nightmare this holiday but she actually hasn't been that bad at all.'

'To be fair, we actually haven't seen that much of her, she's always out and about with her friends. Apart from Maggie and Susan, have you actually met any of these friends of hers?'

'Nope. That's if they exist at all Laney, you know what she's like. For all we know she could be out on her own propping a bar up all day and using Maggie and Susan as an alibi.'

'I suppose so but I must admit, apart from the first couple of days, I haven't really seen her drinking to excess or drunk, have you?'

'No, to be honest I haven't. Perhaps it's finally sunk it what I've been telling her for the last few years.'

'Yeh, and pigs might fly' said Jack rolling his eyes and shaking his head, 'enough talk about Mandy, let's have a go of those inflatables that have been left in the pool. Bagsy Sid gets the unicorn!'

The four of them jumped in the pool and spent the next hour or so swimming, chatting, larking about and generally having a good time. After a lunch of gyros, Greek salad and beers, they went back to the sun loungers and, despite of their good intentions to lay in full sun all day, got under the umbrellas and slept for a couple of hours. When they awoke, they got back into full sun, soaking up the last of the rays, until around half past four when they went back to their rooms to finish packing.

The friends met in the bar on their last evening at the hotel for a couple of cocktails before going out into town for a meal.

'I still haven't seen Mandy' said Andrea looking around the bar. 'She knows it's our last night, you'd think she'd at least come and have a drink with us before going out. But unfortunately that is Mandy to a tee, never thinking!'

'Well it's certainly not going to spoil our evening, whether she joins us or not. Right, one more drink before the off?'

Before they had even ordered their drinks, Mandy came tottering over in her trademark high heels.

'Blimey, talk of the devil, here she comes. Where have you been all day? One minute you were there and the next you'd disappeared. Are you coming out with us this evening or meeting your friends again?'

'Oh, sorry about that, I had to be somewhere. I'm afraid I won't be coming out with you this evening but I'll get you all a drink now though as I've got about half an hour before my taxi turns up. Now, what do you all want?'

Mandy got a round of drinks in and suggested that they all go and sit down somewhere quiet.

'What can't you stand up for long in those heels?' laughed Sid as they took their drinks over to a table.

'No, it's just that I thought you might want to sit down for what I'm going to tell you.'

'Oh my God, what on earth has happened now' said Andrea looking extremely worried. 'I don't think I can take any more surprises on this holiday. Go on then let us have it.'

'It is actually good news, well it is for me anyway. You know I've been going out a lot with Maggie and Susan.'

'Yeh, you've spent a lot of time with them. They do seem really lovely women though.'

'They are really lovely. They both lost their husbands a couple of years ago in a car crash when they were at a golfing trip together in Portugal and since then they've gone everywhere together. We just sort of started chatting at the bar and all three of us just really clicked and now we get on like a house on fire.'

'So, your news is that you've made some friends on holiday?'

'Don't be facetious Jack, it doesn't become you'

'Ooh hark at you just because you've got some new friends.'

'Jack, don't wind her up' said Andrea, 'I'm sure she didn't sit us down just to tell us she's made friends, did you Mandy?'

'No, course I didn't. Right, you most probably know that Maggie and Susan both come from Scotland. Well they've recently bought a place overlooking Loch Lomond that they want to use as a wedding venue. It also comes with accommodation so they can do the whole package. Anyway, whilst we were chatting, they asked me what I do for a living and when I told them I make flower arrangements they asked me if I'd consider working with them. I've had a think about it and seen all the pictures and everything and it really looks lovely. I told them I would give them my final decision tonight but I've already made up my mind to accept, subject to liking what I see when I get there'

'Bloody hell Mandy, Scotland's miles away. I take it you're not going to be commuting every day.'

'Yeh, that'd fun wouldn't it. It'd be alright if I got a Leer Jet to go with the job. No, hopefully I'm going to be moving up there. Nothings' set in concrete yet though. I might get up there and decide it's not for me, but I am excited about it though and it could be the fresh start that I need. What I've done is cancelled my flight home tomorrow and I've booked to go back to Scotland with Maggie and Susan on

Saturday. I'm going to spend a few days up there and get the feel for the place and go from there.'

'Oh my God, I can't believe it' said Andrea looking completely shell shocked, 'you moving to Scotland, I can't believe it. You'll be so far away.'

'It's an hour on the plane Andrea; it's not the other side of the world.'

'I know. What are you going to do about your flat?'

'Well nothing for the time being. There is accommodation that goes with the job so I'll most probably rent my flat out so that I've always got that to fall back if I need it.'

'Well, I'm very shocked' said Andrea hugging her sister, 'but you're right, this could be the best thing for you. I'm really pleased for you and wish you all the luck in the world. Just don't forget your old sister.'

'Yeh, as if I would. I'll still be popping down when I can. You know me; I can't go too long without going to Lakeside! Right, now you're all in the picture, I'd better get going. I said I'd meet Maggie and Susan five minutes ago. We're still going through some ideas for the venue before we fly there on Saturday and let the builders know what they are doing. There's not masses of work to be done on the place, but the sooner it gets done, the sooner we are up and running. If I don't see you tonight when we get back then I'll catch up with you at breakfast in the morning. Have a good last evening.'

With a last hug for all of them, she was out of the door before they could catch their breath.

'Well that was a turn up for the books' said Elaine, 'I certainly didn't expect that.'

'No, it was a bit of a shock' agreed Andrea, 'although to be fair, when she said she had some news, I thought at first she'd met some bloke and was going to shack up with him out here or something so hearing that she is going to work in Scotland is actually quite a relief. At least she's going to keep her flat on so she's got something to come back to if it all goes pear shaped.'

'She'll be fine, Andrea' said Sid, finishing the last of his beer, 'you never know, it might be the making of her. Now where do you fancy eating tonight? I was going to suggest going to the Sunset Grill but that could be a little bit awkward after last week so how about Zorbas seeing as you didn't get to go there when we went last Saturday night?'

'Sounds perfect' said the girls in unison.'

They all finished their drinks and walked over to Zorbas, stopping on the way for Andrea and Elaine to have a quick look in the gift shop opposite.

Once at the restaurant, they were seated almost immediately by the ever helpful Michaelos.

'Good to see you back again' he said to Sid and Elaine, 'and so glad that you bought these two with you. How did the wedding go? Congratulations by the way.'

'Thank you Michaelos, it went really well. In fact it's a dim and distant memory now. It's actually our last night tonight.'

'Oh my God, how fast did that go. Never mind you will soon be back again next year! Now what will you have to drink?'

They ordered their drinks and perused the menu whilst waiting for their order.

'Right seeing as it's my last night' said Sid, putting the menu down, 'I'm going for it and ordering the mixed grill.'

'Have you seen the size of the mixed grill in here' laughed Elaine, 'you'll never eat all that.'

'Maybe not, but I'm going to have a bloody good go. You up for it too Jack?'

'Yeh, what the hell, let's do it. I'm having a starter too.'

'Goes without saying mate. Two baked feta's to start it is then' laughed Sid.

Elaine just looked at him in amazement, shaking her head.

'Well don't expect me to get up with you in the night when you're ill, that's all I'm saying!'

Elaine and Andrea ordered the more sedate mixed souvlaki with a Greek salad to share for starters, whilst the boys ordered the full works. When the mains came up, Jack couldn't believe his eyes.

'Blimey, I didn't think they'd be that big. I'm not sure I'll get through all that.'

'You will' said Andrea, 'or you'll be eating it for breakfast.'

'Okay mum, I'll try my best' laughed Jack as he and Sid started tucking into the enormous plates full of pork fillet, lamb chops, mixed souvlaki, Greek sausage, burger, chicken and gammon, as well as a pile of chips, pitta bread and a side salad.

After quite a struggle, Sid managed to eat most of his plate, leaving only half a sausage, piece of gammon and a few chips. Jack on the other hand was really struggling and was only half way through. Luckily, Elaine and Andrea took pity on him and helped him out, eating most of his chips, a couple of chops and his sausage. At the end of the meal, the plates were almost empty.

'So anyone for dessert?' said Michaelos as he collected the plates.

'You have got to be kidding' groaned Jack as he held his stomach. 'I don't think I'll be eating again for days.'

'Well, I hope you have room for another drink' laughed Michaelos, as he put down a bottle of

Champagne and four glasses. 'This is from me to wish you congratulations on your wedding.'

'Oh, thank you Michaelos' said Andrea, 'that is so kind of you.'

'Yes, it is' agreed Jack, 'you didn't have to do that but we really appreciate it.'

'This is what friends are for' said Michaelos, pouring the Champagne into glasses for them. 'You come here every year and bring your family and friends, this is the least we can do for you.'

They all thanked Michaelos again and raised their glasses to a toast for good luck. Once they had finished their drinks, they paid the bill and said their goodbyes to Michaelos and his staff, promising to see them all again next year. They walked back to the hotel and had a quick look in the bar to see if Mandy was back but, as there was no sign of her and they were all still full from their dinner, they decided to forgo a nightcap and instead headed off to bed and hopefully a good night's sleep ready for going home the next morning.

Friday 19th September

Both Elaine and Sid woke on the last morning refreshed after a great nights' sleep and managed to get dressed and down to breakfast before eight o'clock . They were halfway through their breakfast before Andrea and Jack appeared.

'Blimey, are you two eager to get home or something' said Jack sitting down.

'No, not at all mate' said Sid, 'I just want to get it over and done with now and get home. I hate this bit; waiting around all day for taxis, planes and God knows what else.'

'Yeh, I know how you feel. It'd nice to just walk through a door and find yourself back in your living room wouldn't it?'

'Unfortunately, you can't so you'll just have to put up with it' said Andrea taking ownership of a plate of egg and bacon.

'Bloody hell, how can you lot eat a breakfast like that after the size of the dinners we had last night? My stomach still hasn't got over it.'

'Well if you think I'm going to pay the extortionate prices at the airport for something to eat Jack, you are wrong. So if I was you, I'd get some food down you. It's going to be a long day.'

'I suppose you're right' said Jack, going and getting himself a couple of bacon rolls.

'Have you got everything packed?' asked Elaine

'Near enough. I've just got to put my jeans on and pack these shorts when I get back upstairs. You know you're going home when the jeans go back on. Has anyone seen Mandy this morning, I'd hate to go home without seeing her.'

'I think she's just walking through the door now with, what looks like Maggie.'

The two women walked over to their table and, while Mandy pulled up a chair, Maggie greeted everyone and then excused herself for not staying, explaining that she had to get to the chemists as Susan had a migraine and she desperately needed some tablets. Andrea offered her best wishes on the success of their new venture whilst Jack offered his condolences on having to work with Mandy. Maggie then left Mandy to get some breakfast and say her goodbyes.

'Well that's one thing I won't miss Jack. Your sense of humour.'

'Yeh, right. You know you're going to miss us like mad, you just haven't realised it yet.'

'No, you're right I will miss you all but it's only Scotland. I can come down and you can come and visit me and there's Facebook, Skype, e-mail and phone. I'm hardly going to be cut off from civilisation and it's something I really need to do for myself. Who knows if it will work out but if I don't give it a go, I'll regret it for the rest of my life.'

'Actually Mandy, I'm really proud of you for doing this' said Andrea, putting her hand over Mandy's and starting to well up. 'I must admit I was really shocked at first but I really think this could be the making of you and I'm with you all the way. Now go and get me one of those chocolate croissants before I start blubbing!'

They all sat and finished their breakfast, chatting about Mandy's new venture and the holiday as a whole, until Sid reminded them of the time and they went back upstairs to change and do a final sweep of the rooms. Within half an hour they were back downstairs to book the same two weeks for next year with Christos and Anna who were behind the desk in reception. After saying their goodbyes and thanking them for another wonderful holiday, they sat outside reception with Mandy waiting for their taxi to take them to the airport.

Whilst they sat waiting, Petros and Anita turned up for work and they managed to grab them for 5 minutes and thank them for everything they did to make the wedding go smoothly. After more hugs, kisses and promises to see them next year, Andrea asked if they could pass on their thanks and goodbyes to Eleni and Lambros who they hadn't been able to see.

No sooner had they sat down again than the taxi turned up. The driver somehow managed to load all of their luggage in his car and then, after a teary goodbye to Mandy, they were off to the airport.

Check in was pretty quick and, after having a bit of a spend up in the small duty free shop; they only had around twenty minutes to wait in the departure lounge before their flight was called. Once boarded the plane taxied and took off within a few minutes of its scheduled time and in just over three hours, they were back in Stansted, ready for their onward journey home.

Back Home

Elaine and Sid finally got home after, what seemed like a whole days' travelling. Once they had paid the dog sitter, made a fuss of their fur babies and put the first of many loads of washing on, they finally sat down with a much needed cuppa whilst deciding whether to have Indian or Chinese takeaway for dinner.

'Well, that was soon over wasn't it?' said Elaine, glumly.

'Yeh, I know babes. You wait for it all year and then boom, it's gone. Still look on the bright side, we have already booked for next year and you have to admit, despite all the goings on, we did all have a fabulous time '

'I know we did, but next year is ages away and winter is fast approaching. I don't think I can go that long without another holiday.'

'Well it's a good job I've invited Andrea and Jack round next weekend so we can all decide where we fancy going next. I don't know about you but how does a Caribbean cruise just after Christmas sound?'

'Oh my God, that sounds amazing Sid. What month was you thinking of, because the summer stuff doesn't get into the shops now much before Easter? Oh and I'll have to make sure I don't go too mad at Christmas with all the food. Oh God, I wonder how dressy it is on these ships.'

'Oh no' said Sid his head in his hands, 'here we go again, I wish I'd never mentioned it. I suppose that's all we'll hear about now for months on end, and we haven't even decided where we're going yet. Now give me the phone and I'll order us a shed load of Chinese food. I take it the diet isn't going to start quite yet!'

<u>Acknowledgements</u>

Thank you to the fabulous – Pauline Rose – who has not only done a great job proof reading this book but has also taught me a thing or two about grammar!

Thank you also to my friends in Zakynthos – the Greeks friends who live and work on the island and also our dear English friends who we meet at the same hotel in Kalamaki year after year. Without you there would be no book.

Not forgetting the wonderful people of Zakynthos – thank you for making it the wonderful island that we keep coming back to.

Last, but not least, a great big thank you to my wonderful husband, Dave who supports me emotionally and also gives me great material – unintentionally of course - and my best friend Sally who I use as a sounding board and who also helps me run my two Facebook sites "Eating out in Zante" and "We ♥ The Venus and Kalamaki"

If you enjoyed reading "A Nice Day for a Greek Wedding", you may also enjoy my previous book, "It's all Greek at Sea", an exclusive excerpt of which follows.

After the year from hell, Sally and Mike decide that what they really need is a holiday, so they book themselves on a cruise around the Greek Islands on the luxurious Grecian Princess.

Follow them on a journey of discovery as the ship docks at Zakynthos, Crete and Santorini, to name but a few of the stunning Greek islands they see on their travels. Join them on their shore excursions and sample the delights of local cuisine at beachside tavernas then back on board for some fine dining and great entertainment.

Lots of laugh out loud moments as new found friends get to know each other and find out that some fellow passengers are not quite what they seem!

If you love Greece and/or cruising or just want to read about somewhere warm and sunny, with great food and wine and the chance to make amazing new friends, then this is the book for you.

Chapter One

Sally had never been on a cruise before. She had been on a cross channel ferry from Dover to Calais on the famous "booze cruise", and she had sailed around the shores of Corfu on a "sunset cruise" but she had never been on a vessel the size of the monster that stood in front of her now. In fact she had never even seen a ship the size of the one she was now waiting to board and was starting to worry that maybe a cruise round the Med may not have been such a good idea after all!

The idea of a cruise had grown after Sally had started watching a documentary on TV about the crew on one of the big ships and had fell in love with the idea of sailing around the Med. Her husband, Mike, promised her faithfully that he would take her on a cruise one day and that day came sooner than expected when Mike unexpectedly got made redundant from his job as a Warehouse Manager at a large DIY company.

They decided that they would splash out on a "holiday of a lifetime" with some of his redundancy money, so long as he got another job within a reasonable time. With a bit of luck it would also coincide with Sally's 50th birthday in September, which pleased her no end as it would give her the perfect excuse not to have to throw a party and admit to everyone she was getting old!

Mike had been working for the same company for over 30 years and so got a pretty decent pay off. Although there wasn't any real urgency to find another job, he didn't want to fritter the money away on day to day living, so he started applying for jobs pretty much straight away. But unfortunately, just as he had started getting interviews, everything had to be put on hold after his Dad had a heart attack and he went to stay with him in Norfolk for a while to help him recuperate.

Originally from Essex, Mike's Mum and Dad relocated to Norfolk when Mike was about 12. His Dad, Derek, was offered a job running a machinery plant just outside Norwich and they decided it was too good an offer to turn down. They sold their pokey 2 bed flat in Romford and bought a 3 bedroomed bungalow with beautiful gardens, in a sleepy village not far from the Coast. Both Mike and his Mum, Pat, never really took to the country way of life and Mike moved back down to Essex soon after he had finished college.

Not long after, Derek and Pat split up and Pat also moved back down to Essex. Derek, however, loved the country and fitted in as if he'd lived there all his life. He eventually married again, to Sue, who worked in the offices of his firm. Sue had a daughter, Mia, who was at university in Lincoln. Tragically both Mia and her Mum died in a car accident one night when Sue was taking her back to university after staying with them for the summer holidays. Derek never really got over this and has lived alone ever since, with just his dog for company.

Mike got the call that his Dad had been rushed to hospital after suffering a heart attack, one snowy afternoon in late February and he and Sally drove to the hospital in Norfolk straight away, both of them fearing the worst. Luckily it wasn't a massive heart attack but they kept him in hospital for a couple of days and then advised complete rest for the next few weeks. As Derek lived on his own, Mike decided that it would be best if he stayed in Norfolk to be with him for a few weeks, while Sally came back home for work. After all, it wasn't as if he had to rush back for work or anything and he could still keep applying for jobs while he was taking care of his Dad.

After a couple of weeks at home on her own, Sally decided that, after having had a hectic few months at work she could really do with recharging her batteries and so arranged for a month off without pay to go to Norfolk and keep Mike company. Luckily her boss at the legal firm where she worked, was very understanding and let her have the time off straight away. Derek was home from hospital by then and well on the mend so they mainly spent their days going to the coast and taking Bruno, his faithful cocker spaniel, for long walks along the beach and if the weather wasn't too good they spent their time sitting indoors, watching old movies. By the time Sally's month was up, she felt totally relaxed and re-energised. Little did she know what was just around the corner for her!

They both returned home on the Saturday of the first bank holiday weekend in May, ready for Sally to start back at work on the Tuesday. Whilst in Norfolk, Mike had been offered a job at a rival DIY firm in

Romford and was due to start there as a Senior Warehouse Manager the following week. They were just giving the house a bit of a clean after being away for so long when Sally got a call from her Aunt Jeannie to say that Sally's Mum, June, had collapsed while they were out shopping and was on her way to the hospital. By the time Sally and Mike had got to the Hospital, which was only 15 minutes away, June was in a coma after suffering a massive stroke. They sat with her all night but she never regained consciousness and died early the next morning.

Sally was devastated. Her Mum hadn't even been ill. It was such a shock and she got through the next few days in a complete fog. Mike and his mum, Pat helped her organise the funeral, which thankfully went without a hitch, then Sally completely withdrew into herself. For several weeks she just sat around staring into space, losing hours at a time, hardly sleeping or eating. She wouldn't see a doctor, apart from getting signed off from work, and wouldn't speak to anyone about it, even her good friend Karen, who came round nearly every evening after work to try and cheer her up. Mike was so worried about her but he didn't know what to do.

Her grief finally broke one evening when she and Mike were going through some family photos and videos. A video of a party where June had got slightly tipsy and ended up doing a really bad Karaoke version of Celine Dion's, My Heart Will Go On, finally had Sally laughing. This turned to tears and she eventually cried herself out and slept right round the clock. The next morning she felt as if a mist had lifted and, although she still missed her Mum like crazy, she knew she had to get on with her life.

In her will, June had left everything to Sally, being her only child. Even though Sally would have given it all to have her Mum back, she still had to face facts that she was now quite well off. The family home was worth around £260,000 and there was some shares that June bought when she was working at the bank. They were now worth around £25,000, not to mention her jewellery and other bits and bobs.

Luckily the house sold pretty much as soon as it went on the market, which was one advantage of living in Essex and being so close to the City. As it was sold to a cash buyer and there was no chain, the whole process took just over 4 weeks. Once everything was finalised, and she had paid off the mortgage on her and Mike's house, Sally had around £200,000 in her bank account and a mortgage free house.

When her boss called her and asked when she was thinking of coming back to work, she decided that she would hand her notice in then and there. Her job, as a legal secretary, was quite stressful and, as she didn't actually need the money at the moment, she decided to take time out and get her head together. If, at some point in the future, she wanted to go back to work, she could always get herself a part time job nearer home.

Mike was delighted that she would be at home for the foreseeable future and he suggested that perhaps now was time that they booked that cruise. A bit of sun, sea, good food and wine would do them both the power of good after the last few months that they had just been through. Although if she didn't think she was up to it, Mike was quite happy to just book a week in Cyprus to go and stay with his daughter Lucy, who lived just outside Paphos and had done for a couple of years now, since marrying Pavlos, a Greek Cypriot that she had met on holiday. They both tried to get out there when they could and, now that Sally had given up work, hopefully they could go out more often. Sally agreed that she did need a holiday so they headed off straight away to book something.

When they got to the travel agents, they both headed to the counter to chat to the agent whose badge indicated that he was a "cruise specialist", even though he only actually looked about 16! The baby-faced, travel agent, whose name was Dean, promised to find them the perfect cruise, however, the only one they had available at this short notice was the Greek Island Cruise on the Grecian Princess which sailed out of Corfu on 30th August. Sally and Mike both thought this was perfect and would also coincide with Sally's birthday which was on 10th September. There were only a few decent cabins available so they booked it there and then. With only 2 weeks until they flew out to Greece they started frantically preparing for their holiday.

Preparations were made a lot easier with Sally not being at work but, by the time she had bought a couple of ball gowns, ordered Mike's dinner suit for their formal nights then bought loads more clothes to go away with, ordered some euros, bought all their toiletries and then packed it all, she was frazzled and was definitely in need of a holiday!

Luckily she managed to get booked in for a haircut as she had completely neglected herself the last few months. Her hairdresser cut her chestnut brown hair into a flattering bob that fell in layers, framing her face and making her look years younger than her impending 50th. He completed her look with some delicate blonde highlights that would really stand out once she got in the sun. She left the hairdressers and went straight into her local beauticians where she had her nails done and got waxed within inches of her life. Feeling completely transformed, she had a renewed bounce in her step as she returned home to finish her last minute packing.

Printed in Great Britain
by Amazon

42998465R00199